UNWANTED COMPANY

The instant Frank and Joe fastened themselves into their seats in the front car of the large, empty coaster, the ride began.

The first curves and loops were tame, but as the inclines became steeper and steeper the roller coaster gathered speed. Joe held on tight, so caught up in the fury of the ride that he didn't even notice the first gunshot.

"What was that?" Frank said, startled.

"What?" shouted Joe over the screeching of the roller coaster. Just then, a second bullet ricocheted off the metal railing near his head. "Company!" he yelled at his brother.

Frank and Joe turned to look behind them.

At the end of their car, standing in the last row, was a masked gunman—and he was pointing his gun straight at Joe!

Books in THE HARDY BOYS CASEFILES™ Series

Available from ARCHWAY Paperbacks

UNCIVIL WAR

FRANKLIN W. DIXON

AN ARCHWAY PAPERBACK
Published by POCKET BOOKS

New York London Toronto Sydney Tokyo Singapore

AN ARCHWAY PAPERBACK *Original*

An Archway Paperback published by
POCKET BOOKS, a division of Simon & Schuster Inc.
1230 Avenue of the Americas, New York, NY 10020

ISBN: 0-671-70049-9

First Archway Paperback printing June 1991

10 9 8 7 6 5 4 3 2 1

Cover art by Brian Kotzky

Printed in the U.S.A.

IL 6+

Chapter

1

"PROFESSOR DONNELL! Can I have your autograph?"

Joe Hardy's step faltered as he walked beside Professor Andrew Donnell as he made his way toward the baggage claim area of the Memphis airport. Joe turned to watch a skinny, gawky college-age student in thick glasses and a Tennessee State University sweatshirt run toward them, a small bag dangling from his hand. The student's voice sounded shaky, and he called to the professor with the wild-eyed expression of a fan spotting a movie star.

"Do you know that guy?" Joe asked the professor, eyeing the pale-faced boy rushing up to them. Frank, Joe's older brother, turned, too, to take in the intruder.

"No, don't believe I do," Professor Donnell boomed. He stopped to squint at the boy through his wire-rimmed bifocals.

Joe guessed that the professor didn't mind the public attention. With his shock of thick white hair, pale blue eyes, rumpled tweed sports coat and wrinkled slacks, he appeared as if he had dressed that morning for the role of Famous Professor.

"Well, he sure wants to meet you," Joe remarked. He covered his mouth and tried to stifle a yawn.

Joe and Frank had just flown down to Memphis from their hometown of Bayport to take part in a reenactment of an American Civil War battle for which Professor Donnell was acting as consultant. The professor, who taught in a large New York City university, was an acquaintance of their father, the internationally known detective Fenton Hardy. Fenton had run into the professor at a party, heard about the Memphis reenactment, and suggested it would be a perfect extra-credit history project for his two sons. The brothers' teachers thought it was a great idea, too.

Joe was glad when Donnell agreed to let Frank and him accompany him to Memphis. What better way to study history than to play war for a couple of days? Joe thought.

Now that they were in Memphis, though, Joe only wanted to go to bed. It had been a long flight, there hadn't been enough to eat on the plane, and now some beady-eyed fan was slowing them down.

"You *are* Professor Andrew Donnell, aren't you?" the boy exclaimed abruptly, stopping just in front of them. He spoke with a thick southern drawl, and his voice was deeper than Joe would expect from someone so scrawny.

"Right you are, my boy," Donnell said, smiling at the young man like a lion contemplating his prey. "Forgive me, but have I met you before?"

"Oh, no, sir!" The young man blushed to the roots of his pale hair. He fumbled in his bag and pulled out a hardcover book with the title *Gettysburg Revisited* across its cover. "But I've read just about everything you ever wrote. I heard you were coming into Memphis this afternoon"—the young man stuck the book out toward the pleased professor—"and I was hoping you'd autograph this."

"Certainly, my boy!" the big, brash professor roared, taking the book. "To whom shall I inscribe it?"

"To—to Dennis, sir. Dennis Kincaid."

Joe glanced quizzically at Frank, whose dark eyebrows were raised. He seemed to be surprised. Obviously, he hadn't expected a history professor—no matter how well-known—to be chased down by a fan at an airport.

"Do you always hang out here, hoping your

heroes will wander by?" Joe asked, only half kidding.

"Yes—I mean, no," said Dennis, blushing as he accepted the signed book back from the professor. "I live in Nashville, see. I'm a freshman at State—a history major. I'm going to perform in the reenactment of the Battle of Shiloh here tomorrow. My parents gave me the chance to do it as my birthday present. I'm even staying at Magnolia House."

"The Battle of Shiloh?" Frank said, grinning. "That's what Joe and I are here for."

"What about me?" protested Donnell with good humor. "I'm the star consultant for it, or so I understand." He turned back to Dennis, unwilling to let his admirer go. "Tell me, boy. How'd you recognize me in this crowded place?"

"Th-that's easy, sir," Dennis stammered. He turned the book over, revealing a photograph of the professor on the jacket. "See? It looks just like you."

"I should hope not!" Donnell laughed, obviously flattered. "That picture was taken twenty years ago!"

"And what about you?" Dennis demanded of the brothers. "Why did you come to participate?"

"Extra credit. We need it because we missed a lot of school this year," Frank explained.

"You're being too modest, Frank," said the professor. "Tell the boy why you missed school."

He went on without waiting. "They're famous detectives and were off solving cases."

"Who cares?" said Joe cheerfully, obviously uncomfortable with the praise. "The important thing is that participating in this battle earns us credit for history class. Writing a report about it takes care of English. Figuring the hit-miss ratio for each day aces math. And arguing over who should have won takes care of debate class. Plus, we get a free vacation!"

"This is hardly a vacation for me," the professor snapped. "I happen to be at work on a biography of General Pierre G. T. Beauregard, the leader of the Confederate troops at the battle. I assure you, this battle was no laughing matter."

Joe's grin froze on his face. He shot a puzzled look at his brother but kept his mouth shut.

Dennis seemed to be almost pleased at Joe's reprimand. He cleared his throat and spoke. "Don't you think, sir, that a case could be made that the Battle of Shiloh was General Beauregard's greatest victory? Just because the Yankees claimed to have won doesn't mean—"

"The 'Yankees,' as you call them, didn't *claim* to have won," roared the professor. "They beat that coward Beauregard fair and square, and that's what I intend to prove—once and for all."

Dennis stared, thunderstruck, as the professor wheeled around and took off again to claim his baggage. "Sorry," he whispered to the professor's back.

"Don't worry about it," Joe muttered, heading past the mortified student to catch up with the professor. "My dad warned us that he talks like that all the time."

Still, Joe thought as he hurried after Donnell, that didn't make the professor's rude behavior acceptable.

"Donnell!" A voice called to them from the crowd gathered in the baggage claim area.

"Merriweather!" the professor boomed. Joe spotted a heavyset, nervous-looking young man with slicked-back hair and a closely trimmed beard hurrying toward them. The man's eyes were dark and narrow—ratlike, in Joe's opinion.

"Where's my luggage, man?" Donnell demanded. "We were held up back there. I thought you would have had the bags off the carousel by now."

"They aren't even off the plane, Professor," Merriweather reported, flustered. His dark eyes flicked from the professor to the boys. "Hi. You must be the Hardys. Merriweather's my name. I'm Professor Donnell's graduate assistant. He asked me to accompany him on this trip."

"Not for long, if you don't get our bags," the professor snapped. With that, he stormed off toward a nearby lounge, leaving Joe and Frank with the flustered assistant.

"Does he always treat you like that?" Joe asked.

"What difference does it make?" Merriweather's preoccupied tone surprised Joe. "You have to make allowances for great men."

Frank's eyebrows shot up. "You think Donnell's a great man?"

Merriweather's reverent tone convinced Joe that he had no doubts. "Among Civil War historians, Donnell's the most highly respected, influential thinker of all. He can be as rude as he feels like being."

Joe started to laugh at Merriweather's solemnity but thought better of it. Luckily, the bags had started to arrive, and Merriweather hurried off to retrieve the professor's bags as fast as his chubby legs could carry him.

Behind him, Frank shook his head and Joe chuckled. "I don't get it," Joe said good-naturedly. "So a guy writes a bunch of books on the Civil War. What's so great about that? It's not like he had to invent the story or anything."

"There are plenty of questions about the Civil War, and about this battle in particular," Frank, who was the more studious of the brothers, informed him. "I don't really understand what all the fuss is, either, but maybe we'll find out more tomorrow."

"Yeah," Joe said, rubbing his hands together and grinning. "Rifles, boots, sharp-looking uniforms. I can't wait."

"Just make sure you learn something in the process," Frank chided cheerfully. Then he added, "Look at Merriweather. He's got a whole cart filled with Donnell's stuff. What do you think the professor has in all those boxes?"

"Papers and books," Joe answered. "I asked him when he checked it in New York. He spends a lot of time down here researching and working on his book. He even has an office here."

Joe spotted his and Frank's two garment bags on the luggage carousel. The two boys walked over and swung them off and then plopped them on top of Merriweather's overflowing cart. "Where to now?" Joe asked the assistant.

"We need to catch the shuttle bus to the car rental office," Merriweather replied. He flagged down a porter and instructed him to load everything onto the bus. "Let's go to the lounge to pick up the professor. By the time we get back to the bus, all the bags should be loaded."

"Joe says Donnell has an office in Memphis," Frank said as they entered the lounge. "Where is it?"

"On Tyler Pardee's estate." The assistant peered around the crowded room for his boss. "Pardee's a great guy. He owns the old plantation house outside of town that we're all staying in. He's converted it to a very profitable hotel. He keeps a room on the second floor reserved exclusively for his buddy the professor."

Merriweather spotted Donnell and made his way toward him, explaining to Frank over his shoulder as he moved. "Pardee hosts the reenactment every year."

"Indeed he does," boomed the professor, slapping his assistant on the back. "Wonderful man, Pardee! And incredibly rich! Owns all the land around the Shiloh battlefield. What he didn't use for his hotel he turned into an amusement park—a park with a historic theme, though, so I approve."

"Let's not keep him waiting." Merriweather led them toward the airport exit. "I promised Pardee you'd be there in time for dinner. He eats at six."

"Ah, southerners," Donnell crooned. "Charming, how they eat before sundown."

"Charming," Joe whispered mischievously to his brother as they strolled outside toward the bus, "how Professor Donnell loves food. I don't know about you, but I'm starving."

"Ah, there we are!" The professor spotted the shuttle bus across the lane and down forty feet. The porter was loading the last of his boxes. He started diagonally across the blacktop, ignoring the pedestrian crosswalk. Frank, Joe, and Merriweather followed in his wake.

As he stepped onto the road, Joe became aware of an engine revving. It sounded unusually loud.

"What's that?" he muttered, turning to look to his right. A large blue pickup truck with a Confederate flag covering its front license plate hovered at the end of the lane. The top half of its windshield was tinted dark blue, preventing Joe from seeing into the cab. But the way the engine was being revved made the hairs on the back of his neck stand up in alarm.

"Joe?" he heard Frank say. Too late. The truck was already moving toward Donnell and Merriweather at an alarmingly fast speed.

"Watch out!" Joe leapt toward the professor as Frank charged for Merriweather. The truck careened closer.

It was headed straight for them—and it wasn't slowing down!

Chapter

2

"WHAT ON EARTH—" Merriweather started to protest as Frank knocked him flat to the ground, out of the path of the speeding truck.

Professor Donnell cried out as Joe smashed into him with the full force of his running-back physique. The two of them rolled safely in front of the shuttle bus just as the truck's muddy tires passed inches from them.

"What? I'll b-be—" the professor sputtered as he tried to pull himself to his feet. Joe reached over to help him up.

The porter who had loaded their luggage, the driver of the shuttle bus, and a few other passersby had gathered to stare at the four intended victims. Frank and Merriweather, brushing their pants, joined Joe and the professor.

"Did you see the driver?" Frank asked his brother under his breath.

"No. You?"

Frank shook his head in frustration.

"Are you folks okay?" the shuttle bus driver asked.

"Of course we're all right!" the professor snapped, slapping at the dust on his jacket. "These boys are having trouble controlling their high spirits, that's all. Let's go."

"Wait a minute." Frank stared at the professor, dumbfounded. "My brother just saved your life!"

"Saved my life?" The professor sniffed haughtily. "Ridiculous. My life wasn't in danger."

"But the truck!" Frank turned to Merriweather, but the assistant just stared at the ground and shifted his weight from one foot to the other. The watching crowd backed away slightly, as if they were in the presence of crazy people, and murmured among themselves.

"That truck would've run right over you if Joe hadn't pushed you out of the way!"

"Nonsense." The professor brushed past the brothers and climbed onto the bus.

Furious, Frank thought about pursuing the professor but realized it would be useless to argue with him.

Shaking his head, Frank joined Joe. Merriweather, still stunned, followed behind.

"Who would have tried to run us down?" Frank asked Joe as they approached the bus.

"I was wondering the same thing," Joe admitted. "The only person we've even talked to here was that Dennis Kincaid."

"Why would he want to run us over?"

Joe shrugged his shoulders and grinned ruefully. "We embarrassed him, maybe?"

Frank laughed. "Maybe it was just an accident," he said finally. But he knew that neither he nor Joe believed that.

By five-fifteen the foursome was driving in a rented car through the rolling green hills of the Memphis countryside, each lost in his own thoughts.

Finally Frank could stand the tense silence no longer. He leaned forward from the backseat and asked the professor in a polite voice, "Sir, could you tell us about the Battle of Shiloh."

The professor's face instantly brightened. "Certainly, Frank. It began, on this land we're riding through, back on April sixth, 1862. It was the largest, most devastating battle to that date in the Civil War—some twenty thousand men killed in two days of fighting—and it killed any hope on either side that the war would be over quickly."

"Why did Dennis say the South might have won the battle?" Joe's mind was still on the college student.

The professor's face twitched in annoyance. "Actually," he explained, "the South *was* victorious the first day. But the second day, April seventh, General Grant counterattacked with fresh reinforcements and won. Unfortunately for the rebels, the battle enabled the Union forces to advance north and capture Memphis, thus effectively controlling the state of Tennessee. History places the victory squarely in the Union camp."

"And General Beauregard led the Confederate forces?" Frank asked.

"Brilliant soldier," the professor said, nodding. "But he made some major errors at Shiloh."

"Like what?"

The professor blinked. "First, he should have attacked on the evening of the first day of battle when he had the Union on the ropes. But instead he chose to rest for the night."

"What else?"

"The next day," Donnell continued, "when he might have made a tougher stand against the North, he chose to retreat." He readjusted his jacket. "Many people blame old Beauregard for the South's defeat that day. I count myself among them."

"Where'd the fighting take place, exactly?" Joe asked eagerly.

"Right out there." The professor nodded out the window. "That's the Tennessee River. To the west is the Shiloh National Military Park.

And here to the east are Mr. Pardee's mansion and Rebel Park, which is nearly twice the size of the national park, I'm told.''

"Wow." Joe craned his neck to see past his brother's shoulder. "Not bad."

Frank spotted a large, ornate wrought iron gate with the words *Magnolia House* expertly woven into its design where it arched over the paved private drive. The gate swung open automatically as Merriweather guided the car off the main road and onto the estate.

"This is an amusement park?" Joe gazed around at the well-tended lawns, magnolia trees, and the pine forest that lined the property.

"Of course not," Merriweather scoffed. "These are the grounds of the plantation house. Rebel Park is on the right, past those trees. The annual reenactment takes place just beyond that."

Joe whistled. "Sounds like a lot of land."

"Certainly is." The professor smiled.

"Wow. Look." Frank nudged his brother in the ribs, then pointed at the enormous, white-columned mansion that swung into view as the car rounded the last curve in the long drive. It was a classic, three-story plantation house with a veranda that wrapped around the two lower stories and enormous windows looking out onto the manicured lawns. "Some hotel, huh?"

As Merriweather shut the engine off, a uniformed valet approached the car. "Welcome, Dr. Donnell," he said. "Mr. Pardee is waiting for you in the library. We'll take care of your bags.''

Frank and Joe followed the professor and his assistant into the house. Frank was even more impressed with the inside of the mansion than the outside. The ceiling of the foyer soared thirty feet above the marble floor. Richly varnished wood paneling made the huge space seem warm and cozy.

In the middle of the lobby the marble floor gave way to a marble staircase that rose majestically to the second floor. "Come on," Frank said, eager to explore the rest of the house. He led the way up the stairs behind the professor and Merriweather.

As they reached the top of the stairs they could already hear the professor loudly greeting his host in one of the rooms at the end of the hall. Frank and Joe entered behind him and found themselves inside a large library with a huge fireplace and floor-to-ceiling bookcases.

"Good to see you again, Andrew," a man was saying to the professor, shaking his hand. "Welcome back to Magnolia House."

Frank, watching their slender, middle-aged host, smiled to himself. Pardee was a friendly-looking man, with well-trimmed brown hair that had turned white at the temples and intelligent, pale green eyes.

"You must be Joe and Frank Hardy," Pardee added, reaching out to shake their hands. "The professor's told me about you two, not to mention that dad of yours. I'm pleased to make the acquaintance of two such clever detectives.''

"We're on a sort of learning vacation here,'' Frank said, smiling at him.

"We hope so, at least,'' his brother added in a low voice.

"Good,'' replied Pardee. "Because it so happens that you have to attend a dinner party for all the folks participating in tomorrow's battle down at the amusement park. Better two teenagers at a party than a couple of ace detectives, don't you agree? But first''—he winked conspiratorially at Frank and Joe—"I've got a surprise for Andrew.''

Frank watched as Pardee walked toward the fireplace. On the wall above it hung an impressive array of knives, sabers, and bayonets, which Frank logically guessed dated to the Civil War. Pardee took a saber from the wall and handed it to his friend. "Look at this,'' he said to the professor.

Frank watched as Donnell turned the saber over in his hands, inspecting the shiny blade and ornately carved handle with growing disbelief. "It can't be,'' he said at last to Pardee. "When you told me about this, I didn't really believe you had come up with it.''

Pardee beamed. "Well, sir, I did. This here's the genuine article.''

"What is it?'' Frank asked.

The professor slowly continued to shake his head. "Tyler claims this is the saber that General Beauregard carried into the Battle of Shiloh."

"I do more than claim," Pardee retorted. "Look here."

He pointed to the base of the blade. Both Frank and the professor peered closer. Frank made out the name *P. G. T. Beauregard* engraved in tiny letters.

"Had it authenticated at Tennessee University a week ago," Pardee said. "One of my men found it when we were excavating for all those new rides we're putting in at the park."

The professor shook his head, gazing at the valuable saber. "Better to be lucky than rich," he said.

"To tell you the truth," said Pardee, grinning widely, "it's better to be both."

He took the saber from the professor and replaced it on the wall. "Now we'd better get down to that party."

Though separated from Magnolia House by the tall wrought iron fence, Rebel Park was only about a hundred yards from the mansion. As Frank and Joe accompanied the others along the brick walk to the park's entrance, they could hear a band playing in the distance, as well as the sounds of talk and laughter.

"How long has your family had Magnolia House?" Frank asked as they approached a gate to the park.

Pardee grinned. "Depends on who you talk to, I reckon," he said. "My people first settled this particular land back in the late 1700s. Been adding bits and pieces ever since. The professor here doubts my claim, but after all, possession *is* nine-tenths of the law."

The professor cleared his throat, seemingly annoyed, and Pardee laughed. Frank wondered what the hotel owner meant, but there was no time to ask. They had reached the entrance to the park. On the other side of the gate stood an enormous red-and-yellow tent that Pardee said housed the band, dinner, and most of the guests. Frank grinned at Joe's eager expression. Joe had obviously forgotten how tired he was and was now ready to party.

"Ah, gentlemen!" Pardee called out to several men standing just outside the entrance to the tent. He led his guests toward them, saying expansively to the professor, "About time I introduced you to a few of our more fascinating locals.

"Andrew Donnell, meet Martin Crowley," Pardee said, gripping the arms of both men. "Andrew, Martin's read every one of your books. He's our recorder of deeds in Memphis, so I guess he has a taste for history."

"I know Martin quite well already," the professor replied, beaming at the round-shouldered, pasty-faced man in the three-piece suit. "We've had a number of conversations regarding my new book. In fact, I'm considering acknowledging you in it, Martin.''

"Really, Andrew?'' the man said tentatively. "I didn't realize I'd been so helpful.''

Frank noticed annoyance flash across Pardee's face, but he quickly recovered and turned toward the other two men.

"Okay, then, let me introduce Wayne Robinson of Macon, Georgia, and our own Wesley Hart,'' he said to the professor. "Two more loyal readers.''

Donnell smiled and bowed slightly to the two men.

Frank studied them. Robinson was a short, paunchy man with a bulbous nose and squinty blue eyes. Hart, younger and more muscular, had the hooded eyes of a hungry hawk.

"Gentlemen,'' Donnell said, "it's always a pleasure to meet fans. The name Wayne Robinson rings a bell.''

Before Robinson could answer, Hart said to the professor, "Just because a man reads your book doesn't mean he believes what you write.''

The professor's smile faded. "Indeed,'' he said, straightening up. He seemed to brace himself for an argument.

But before Hart could continue, they were interrupted by Joe, who muttered, "Wow!'' in a too-loud voice.

They all turned to watch Joe smiling at a slender girl in a simple summery blouse and skirt who was heading toward the group. Her long red hair was lifted off her shoulders in the slight breeze. Frank couldn't help but notice how attractive she was. Uh-oh, he thought. Joe's just found his own fascinating local.

"Daddy, I just called for more soda water," the girl said to Tyler Pardee in a soft, southern-accented voice. Then she noticed the Hardys. Her face, which was splashed with freckles, broke into a wide grin.

"You're the Hardys, aren't you?" she asked, putting her hand out. "I'm Jennifer Pardee. Daddy's told me all about you."

Frank waited for his brother to take Jennifer's hand, but the girl had Joe forgetting what to do. Frank grinned and shook the girl's hand instead. "I'm Frank," he said to Jennifer. "This dumbfounded blond, blue-eyed loon here is Joe."

"Pleased to meet you, Frank and Joe," Jennifer drawled. "Welcome to my amusement park. If y'all want free tickets to the rides later, just let me know."

"*Your* amusement park?" Joe managed to say, his voice cracking just a little.

Pardee and the other men chuckled. "You heard right," Pardee said, putting an arm around his daughter's shoulders. "Jennifer's been working here since she was thirteen. When she turned eighteen last month, I handed the reins over to her."

"Not the whole thing," Jennifer protested,

blushing. "I run the ideas department. Party schemes, new concessions, promotions and stuff. Daddy still handles the money end."

"Not for long, though," Pardee said proudly. He turned toward Jennifer. "Why don't you show the boys around, honey?"

"Sure!" Jennifer smiled at Frank and Joe.

To Joe's relief, Jennifer asked them if they'd rather eat first. While they loaded their plates at the buffet, she described the park's rides, games, horse rentals, and Civil War–related shows.

"How do you manage to run all this and go to school, too?" Joe wanted to know as they chose a table and sat down to eat.

She smiled. "I'm used to it, I guess. Other girls wait on tables or take piano lessons after school. I call the repairman for the merry-go-round. Of course, this weekend I'll be especially busy. The battle reenactment always attracts lots of folks to Rebel Park."

Frank was about to ask her another question when a commotion near the entrance to the tent distracted him. Frank recognized the voice of Professor Donnell.

"Get your hands off me, man!" he shouted. His voice was loud enough to cut through the party conversation. The band members, who had stopped for a short break, all turned to stare at the two men from their place on the stage.

"You don't tell me what to do!" Wesley Hart shouted back at the professor. Frank wondered where Pardee and Robinson were as he saw the younger man push the professor in the chest. The professor staggered backward, causing several onlookers to scream.

"Stop that or I'll call the police!" the professor shouted wildly. Frank stood, ready to run to help the professor. But he was too far away to stop Hart from attacking again.

As Frank, Joe, and Jennifer watched, Hart pushed the professor once more. As the older man fell backward onto the ground, Hart stood over him, shouting, "I'll kill you, Donnell! I swear I will!"

Chapter

3

INSTANTLY JOE AND FRANK sprang into action. They pushed through the crowd to where the professor sat stunned on the ground and pulled the red-faced attacker away from him.

Frank, holding one of Hart's arms, demanded, "What's this all about?"

"None of your business." Hart glared at the professor, whom Joe was helping back to his feet for the second time that day.

"It was nothing, dear boy," Donnell said, glaring at Hart. "A mere misunderstanding."

"Misunderstanding?" Hart shouted. "I understand perfectly! You're filling your book with a pack of lies about General Beauregard. You ought to be shot!"

"Hey, watch it." Joe held up his hands. "It's

24

a free country, right? He can write what he wants.''

"He can't tell lies and get away with it," said Hart. With that, he turned and stomped off.

Joe looked around. Now that the argument was over, the other guests had gone back to their celebrating again. The band struck up a good dance tune, and everyone ignored the pro fessor and the two brothers.

"What's going on here?" Joe asked Frank after Pardee rushed up and took the professor to a table, where they were now sitting.

Frank shook his head. "I know one thing. This is no get-together of the Andrew Donnell Fan Club. Hart may not be the professor's only problem," he added quietly. "Look, there's that Dennis Kincaid—over there, talking to Mr. Hart. Kincaid seems to be as angry as Hart is."

"Thank goodness you boys were here." Joe jumped at the sound of Jennifer's soft voice in his ear. He turned to find her standing behind him. "That Wesley Hart has always had a terrible temper," she confessed. "People like him give the South a bad name."

"And what about people like you?" Joe said with a smile, everything else instantly vanishing from his mind.

Jennifer took his arm and began to lead him out of the tent. "Southerners like me take good care of their guests at parties. And I'm going to give you a tour of Rebel Park."

She turned back to Frank. "Would you like to come along?" she asked, smiling welcomingly.

Frank grinned. Whether he wanted to or not, Joe would kill him if he ruined his get-together. "No, thanks," he said. "I'll hang out here and eat a bit more, then I'll turn in early. It's been kind of a long day."

The next morning Frank awoke to a dark room and a shrieking alarm clock. Sitting straight up in bed, he slammed the clock with one hand.

Across the room he saw Joe lying half on and half off his bed, oblivious to the noise. Joe was still dressed in the clothes he had worn the day before. Frank shook his head, remembering how he had awakened around midnight when Joe had come tiptoeing in.

"Get up, little brother." Frank tossed a pillow at Joe. "Don't say I didn't warn you."

"Mmmph." Joe shoved the pillow off his face and sat up, blinking sleepily. "Tell 'em to have the war without me, okay?"

Frank laughed as he got out of bed and started dressing. "No way. The troops meet in the dining room in twenty minutes."

Joe yawned and stretched, then slowly climbed out of bed and went to the closet, where his dark blue Union uniform was hanging. "How come I'm North and you're South?" he asked.

Frank was studying himself in the mirror. Confederate gray was a good color for him, he

26

decided. "I'm not sure how they divided up the sides. You know what they said about the Civil War, though, don't you? Brother against brother?"

"Yeah." Joe grinned. "Let's fight."

Leading the way down to the dining room, Joe was surprised to see more than four hundred men crammed into the huge room, and dressed in authentic-looking Civil War uniforms, the colors equally divided between gray and blue. He spotted the professor wearing the uniform of a Southern general, with Merriweather beside him, dressed in Union blues.

"Good morning, boys," roared the professor when he saw Joe and Frank standing in the doorway. "I trust you slept well."

"We did." Frank glanced at Joe, who was stifling a yawn. "Did you sleep well?"

"Sure." Joe led the way to the professor's table. "But then, I always sleep well. Clear conscience. Clean living. Works every time."

"How about you, Robert?" Frank asked Merriweather amiably as he and his brother sat down at the table.

Merriweather didn't answer right away. Frank decided the assistant was either still half asleep or lost in thought.

"Oh—er, fine," Merriweather said at last. "Fine, I guess."

"Well, I feel much better," Joe said as a waitress served him and Frank heaping plates of scrambled eggs, grits, bacon, fried potatoes, and biscuits. "Nice to know that no matter which side you're on, you still get fed right before the battle."

The others were too busy eating to answer. In fact, they downed their meals in near silence. As they were finishing their breakfast, Tyler Pardee appeared at the front of the room.

Joe glanced up from his breakfast long enough to notice that Pardee wore the uniform of a Union general. I guess I'll have to address him as sir for the next couple of days, he told himself.

Pardee's speech interrupted his thoughts. "Good morning, men," the slender man was saying, smiling broadly at his guests. "I hope you're enjoying your breakfast at Magnolia House. We do our best to please you folks going into battle. In any case, rest assured it's better than the food those first soldiers—on both sides—had to eat that morning at Shiloh."

The crowd murmured its agreement. Joe glanced around at the attentive faces—more alert now than they had been before they were served.

"The reenactment is set to begin at dawn," Pardee continued. He checked his pocket watch. "That's in about an hour. We'll leave here in ten minutes. Those of you in Union uniforms will follow me. Confederate soldiers are under

Professor Andrew Donnell's supervision. Stand up, Professor.''

The professor rose and nodded to the men, then sat down again.

"There's a room just off the foyer where you'll pick up your rifles and blank ammunition," Pardee said. "Sheriff Bradley Walker and I will be monitoring the ammunition, to be on the safe side. If you run out of cartridges during the day, there's a supply tent on the battlefield not far from Shiloh Church where you can get more. That tent is being supervised by Wesley Hart."

Wesley Hart seemed to be almost cheerful as he stood up across the room from Joe and Frank.

"Okay," Pardee concluded. "Now, finish your breakfast and we'll see you outside the hotel."

Shortly before dawn Joe found himself with more than two hundred other blue-uniformed actors in tents at the site of the Shiloh battlefield. Through the open flaps of the tent, Joe could see Tyler Pardee surveying the scene from atop an enormous white horse. A crowd of spectators shivered in the chilly morning air.

Joe also spotted Robert Merriweather wandering back and forth in the predawn light as though searching for something or someone. Joe wondered if he should ask the assistant whether he could help him when a voice interrupted his thoughts.

"Hey, remember me?"

At the sound Joe turned quickly and stepped outside into the gray morning. The voice belonged to Dennis Kincaid.

"Sure," Joe said, controlling the urge to cross-examine the student about pickup trucks and his real feelings about Professor Donnell. "What are you doing in a Yankee uniform?"

Kincaid's smile faded, and he looked down, flustered. "Well, er, they didn't really give me a choice. How about you?"

"Ditto." Joe was becoming restless. "What happens now?"

The college student scanned the field for a moment. "Well," he said at last. "When the sun comes up, I reckon the South will rise again."

Meanwhile Frank and the rest of the Confederate troops were lining up just behind the top of a bluff near the Union camp, preparing to attack. Frank hunched down in the cold air, watching his breath form clouds that floated lazily away.

"Nervous?" said the soldier beside him.

Frank nodded.

"This your first battle?"

"Yeah," Frank answered.

"Don't worry. These blanks just give a little sting. Can't hurt nobody unless you shoot 'em at point-blank range."

Frank was about to say that that was just what he'd been telling himself, when he realized he'd seen his neighbor before. "Hey, you're Wayne Robinson, aren't you? We met last night."

Robinson grinned and was about to answer, but just then the ball of the sun broke over the horizon and Frank watched as Professor Donnell, riding a chestnut mare, gave the signal to charge. Instantly Frank joined his fellow soldiers and hurtled downhill, shouting, toward the Union camp.

To Frank's gratification, the Union soldiers were caught completely by surprise. But it didn't take them long to regroup as the first wave of Confederate foot soldiers descended on them. Within minutes, resounding cannon blasts were exploding among the rebel troops.

"Take shelter!" Frank heard someone yell. He dove behind a large rock and waited, while others hid behind trees and in ruts in the ground. The cannon fire ceased, and Frank and his fellow soldiers ran out from their hiding places to attack.

Frank wasn't prepared for the noise of battle. The two armies faced each other across less than fifty feet of dust and filled the air with the explosions of four hundred rifles at once.

At first Frank thought he would never get through the day. He wondered if there was some way he could quit the reenactment early. He also wondered how the real soldiers had managed to drag themselves through battle after battle for the many years of the war.

After thirty minutes Pardee signaled the Northerners to pull back. Frank and the other Confederate soldiers also withdrew to the steep banks of the Tennessee River. Frank hoped that would be the end of the fighting for a while, but instead the professor ordered his troops to attack.

Not my lucky day, Frank thought gloomily as he prepared his rifle for the onslaught.

The fighting by the river was even worse than before. Dust filled the air. Cannonballs splashed into the river and drenched the soldiers who clung to the riverbank. The weary fighters grew increasingly clumsy as they aimed their heavy rifles at one another.

At some point Frank saw Professor Donnell himself struggling at the bottom of the riverbank nearby. "Fantastic, eh, boy?" he shouted to Frank. "This is where General Johnston was killed the first day of fighting and Beauregard became the sole commander. Beauregard might have changed history if he had fought on instead of pulling back!"

Before Frank could answer, the shooting started again. The professor turned away and struggled up the riverbank, waving his rifle and shouting at his men.

Frank watched him, startled. Something was wrong. There was the same stench of gunpowder, the same clouds of smoke that he had been smelling and seeing all day. Frank rubbed his eyes. Something was different, but what?

Then he realized that a tree beside Donnell was suddenly sporting a hole. He could see splinters spraying out of it.

"Wait!" he shouted after Donnell.

But Frank could see that Donnell had no intention of stopping the battle now.

"Professor! Wait! Stop the—"

Frank never finished his sentence. He stopped in his tracks atop the riverbank. All around him he could hear the high whine of bullets. He could see dust flying as the shells hit the ground around him.

Suddenly he felt something hit him, and he put a hand to the back of his head.

He'd been shot!

Chapter

4

"OH, MAN, are you okay?"

Frank, facedown in the mud of the riverbank, was dimly aware of someone running over to help him. Hands flipped him over roughly. Then he was staring into a pair of terrified brown eyes. He had never seen this Confederate soldier before.

"Oh, gee, I got one of my own men," the soldier moaned. Frank grinned, astonished at how seriously the stranger was taking this.

"But it was only a blank, right?" the soldier said, trying to convince himself. "You must have been pretty close to me, but you'll be okay, right? It's not even bleeding."

"Naw, it's just a bruise." Frank shifted his gaze and saw another soldier in gray standing over them. His rifle rested over one shoulder, and he looked more like an insurance salesman than a soldier, Frank thought.

"You just startled the kid, that's all," the man added to calm their frightened colleague.

Frank started to laugh. "That's the great thing about reenactments," he said. "The bullets aren't real."

Suddenly he remembered. The bullets! They *were* real! He sat bolt upright. Something had to be done!

"Professor!" he yelled, struggling to get to his feet while the two soldiers struggled to hold him back so he could rest. "Professor Donnell!"

"What's he saying?" asked the soldier who had hit him with the blank. "Ain't Donnell Union?"

"No, he's one of us," said the insurance salesman. He pointed to a rise about twenty feet away. "There he is, right there."

Frank spun in that direction and spotted the professor astride his chestnut mare. His back was to Frank, and he obviously hadn't heard him over the noise of the gunfire.

"Professor!" Frank broke free of the soldiers and ran toward the gray-suited general. "Listen to me!"

Miraculously, Donnell heard him. He turned in his saddle and fixed Frank with an angry glare.

"What?" he shouted impatiently, cupping a hand to his ear.

Frank started to answer, but his foot caught on a tree root and he stumbled slightly, catching himself on his hands before he hit the ground face first. When he raised his eyes, it was too late.

Frank watched as a bullet caught the professor in the chest, sending him spinning off the back of the horse. The chestnut mare reared and whinnied and took off at a gallop.

"Get the horse!" Frank shouted back over his shoulder at his fellow soldiers and stumbled forward to the wounded professor. At the first sight of the bleeding wound, both sides had stopped fighting. Frank's words to get the horse rung out in an eerie silence. An instant later a hundred men ran forward to help the professor.

It was too late. Frank searched for any sign of life. There was none. In the distance he could hear the sound of an ambulance siren. He just stared at the dead professor, stunned into silence, until the paramedics arrived to take the body away.

"Frank!" Frank became aware of Joe beside him as ranks of soldiers moved past them to watch Donnell's body being loaded into the back of the ambulance.

"It's okay, Joe," Frank managed to say. "I mean, I'm fine. It's the professor."

"We all saw. What happened?"

"That's what we want to know, son."

Frank looked up to see a pale, grim-faced

Tyler Pardee approaching them with an equally grim-faced companion also in Union blue.

"Frank, this is Sheriff Walker," Pardee said, his tone all business. "He has some questions for you."

"Okay, son," the sheriff said. "Just tell me what happened."

Eager to cooperate, Frank related the events of the last few minutes. He mentioned the flurry of real bullets and the blank in the back of his head.

"Hmm. Anything else?" the sheriff asked, scribbling notes in a pad he had pulled from the pocket of his uniform.

"Nothing I can think of." Frank rubbed the back of his head, which was still sore. "Before I could stop him, he was dead."

"Any idea where the shots came from?"

Frank shook his head. "I'm just not sure."

The sheriff looked around the site and shook his head. "Okay, son," he said, slapping Frank on the shoulder. "Thanks for your help. Stick around the hotel for the next couple of days, okay? I might need to question you further. I'll be over there or here most of the day to continue the investigation."

By early that evening news of Donnell's death had spread through town. Magnolia House was swarming with reporters and curiosity seekers, not to mention most of the four hundred soldiers. Joe and Frank had showered and changed into civilian clothes. Now they were standing at the top of the marble stairs, watching the pandemonium in the foyer below.

"I still can't believe Donnell's dead," Joe said, shaking his head.

"I know what you mean," Frank said. "The scene keeps flashing in my mind. If only I hadn't tripped, Donnell might still be—"

"You can't be so hard on yourself," Joe said, cutting off his brother's sentence.

"I know," Frank said thoughtfully. "While I was showering I was thinking that we didn't tell the sheriff about the pickup truck or that fight Donnell had with Wesley Hart."

Joe's eyebrows shot up. "That's right," he said. "He'd probably want to know about those incidents. I think we should head for the library and have a little talk with the sheriff."

"A pickup truck?" Sheriff Walker's skepticism showed on his face, even in the dim light from the fire in the fireplace. It was too hot for a fire, Frank reflected, shifting uncomfortably in the heat. But Sheriff Walker obviously was enjoying the luxury of his temporary surroundings. April or not, he was going to use the fireplace.

"Yes, sir. A blue truck with a Confederate flag on the front license plate," Frank replied. He watched the sheriff shift his weight in the big leather chair behind the library desk. "We couldn't identify the driver. But if my brother, Joe, hadn't knocked the professor out of the way, that truck would have mowed him down."

"Hmm." The sheriff frowned down at his notes. "Anything else, then?"

Joe stepped forward to tell the sheriff about the fight that had taken place at the party the evening before. The sheriff had been there, and he was soon nodding impatiently, indicating that he had witnessed it, too. Several others had mentioned the argument to him also.

"Wesley Hart's a hothead," he said, putting his pen down and leaning back in the chair.

"Enough of a hothead to carry out his threat?" asked Joe.

The sheriff shook his head, frowning, but failed to meet Joe's insistent gaze. "I guess I'll have to check it out," he said at last. "I sure don't have much else to go on."

The boys sat in uncomfortable silence for a moment. Then the sheriff stood, reaching out to shake their hands. "Thanks for your help," he said. "I'll let you know if I have any more questions."

"Uh, Sheriff," Joe stammered, shaking the man's hand. "We were wondering, Frank and I. . . ."

"Wondering what?"

Frank stood up, facing the older man. "Would you mind if we hung around while you questioned the others?" he asked. "We feel kind of responsible for what happened. I mean, we didn't know it was going to happen or anything, but—"

"We're pretty good at investigations," Joe put in. "It seems that if we couldn't prevent Dr. Donnell's death, at least we can help catch the killer."

The sheriff hesitated, eyeing the boys. Finally he cleared his throat. "Don't go blaming yourselves," he said. "Doesn't seem like there was much you boys could have done. And who knows, maybe it was just an accident after all."

"You don't really believe that, do you?" Joe protested.

The sheriff sighed. "At the moment I don't believe anything," he said.

Two hours later Frank had to ask himself if he and Joe weren't useless in the investigation. All day they'd listened to witnesses tell the same stories of seeing Donnell hit during the battle and of hearing the argument at the party the night before. And as far as Frank could tell, no one had offered a single clue as to who the killer might be. No one had seen Hart anywhere near the professor. In fact, no one had seen Hart all that day.

Frank glanced at Joe, who appeared to be half asleep on a loveseat. Frank knew his brother felt as bad as he did about the professor. But he also knew how hungry he must be by now. Maybe the two of them should take a break, he thought.

Go downstairs for dinner. Maybe the food would recharge their mental batteries and they'd come up with a new idea.

"Wesley Hart," the sheriff said. Frank's head jerked up. Hart had just been let into the room and was crossing the carpet to shake the sheriff's hand. He still wore his Confederate uniform and looked pale and muddy—and scared, Frank realized. He must have understood how bad his threats from the night before made him look.

"What're they doing here?" he asked, nodding toward Frank and Joe.

"Helping with the investigation," the sheriff said smoothly. "Now, sit down, Wesley, and tell me what you were doing during the battle. No one can recall even seeing you there."

"I was in the ammo tent." Hart scowled at the boys, then sat down grudgingly in a leather-upholstered chair. "Handing out blanks, stocking cannons. I got a dozen people who can back me up."

"Can you give me a list of names?" the sheriff asked.

"You heard me," Hart said belligerently. "Give me paper and a pencil and I'll write 'em down."

Frank stood up abruptly. "Thanks for letting us stay, Sheriff," he said to Walker. "I think Joe and I will go downstairs and have a look around."

The sheriff glanced up at him. "Suit yourselves," he said curtly.

As he left the overheated library, Frank heard Joe hurrying to catch up with him.

"What's up, Frank?"

"Nothing," Frank muttered, walking slowly down the hall. "Hart wasn't going to spill anything, that's all. That is, if he had anything to spill. I figured we could spend our time more wisely by checking out the other men who were in the field."

"Good idea." Joe licked his lips, and Frank grinned, knowing he was dreaming of food again.

"You go down the back stairs," Frank said. "They lead directly to the dining room and kitchen. I'll take the front stairs and talk to the guys in the foyer."

"Yes, sir!" Joe saluted, then turned and jogged down the hall toward the back stairs. He was hungry and in a hurry. As he raced down the dark, narrow staircase, Joe heard something behind him. It sounded like the door at the top of the staircase slowly opening and closing.

He turned, but saw nothing—it was too dark. He also heard nothing more. Must have been my stomach growling, Joe thought to himself.

But as he continued down the wooden stairs, a leg suddenly swung down from behind him and kicked him on the back of the neck. Joe had no time to react as he flipped forward and fell into the long darkness.

Chapter

5

JOE WAS FLYING, out of control. He screamed once and grabbed for the banister, but got nothing but a fistful of air.

Throwing his arm wide, he reached again and got a piece of it this time. He slowed his fall enough to save himself from landing head-first on the stone floor in the hall at the bottom of the stairs. He heard the door at the top of the stairs open and close as someone called out, "Joe!"

A door banged open in the back hall right beside Joe. Frank was standing in the doorway, the light from the dining room behind him. "You okay?" he asked.

"I'll live," Joe said, leaning against the wall. Frank checked his head for cuts and bruises.

"What happened?"

"All I know is, someone or something drop-kicked me halfway down the stairs."

"Maybe we'd better stick together after all," Frank muttered, leading the way into the dining room.

"I'm for that," said Joe, massaging a sore spot on his shoulder. "Where do we start?"

Frank hesitated in the doorway. "How about Dennis Kincaid?" he said. "He said he was staying here at the hotel, remember. I have a couple of questions to ask him."

"No food first?" Joe asked as they moved through the large room, which smelled of roast beef, fried chicken, and hush puppies.

"Tell you what, Joe. Ask Dennis some nice sharp questions and dinner's on me."

Dennis Kincaid answered the door of Room 311 on the second knock. Joe noticed that he didn't seem at all surprised to see the Hardys.

"I wondered when you guys would get around to looking me up," he said as he led them into his room and motioned them to sit on the small sofa.

"What made you think we'd want to see you?" Joe asked.

Kincaid sat on the bed. "Makes sense, doesn't it? I mean, you saw the professor insult me at the airport. You might figure I could have killed him for that."

"Is that a confession?" Frank asked.

"Of course not. I'm not a killer."

"Fine," Joe said. "Then what can you tell us about the shooting?"

"Not much." Kincaid leaned back against the headboard of the bed. Joe reflected that he was remarkably calm for someone whose hero had just been murdered and for someone who might easily become a suspect. "As you know, I was on the Northern side, same as you," he said to Joe. "And it was loud. I was having a great time, to tell you the truth. It was my first time at a reenactment. I had never shot a muzzle-loader before. But I was on the edge of the battle when the professor got killed. I didn't see anything. Some people said maybe it was a spectator."

"Somebody would probably have noticed if a spectator had a gun," Frank pointed out.

"One more question," Joe persisted, leaning forward. "Last night, at the party, after Wesley Hart threatened to kill the professor, you and he were talking together."

"So?"

"So, what were you talking about?"

Kincaid blinked. "Nothing," he said. "I mean, I don't remember."

"Don't remember, or won't remember?" asked Frank.

Dennis's eyes darted from one Hardy to the other nervously. "Look, I'm telling you, I didn't do anything wrong."

45

"Then tell us what you and Hart were talking about." Joe's voice was starting to rise.

Frank reached out to calm his brother. "You aren't in any trouble—yet," he said to Kincaid. "Anything you tell us will be confidential. But a man has been killed, and your help in finding out who did it is vital."

Joe waited, listening to the intense silence in the room, for Kincaid to speak.

When he finally spoke, it was in little more than a whisper. "I don't want to get anybody in trouble."

"Professor Donnell is dead." Joe was almost seething.

"It might make you feel better to tell us," Frank said. "We can help you."

Kincaid said, "After you broke up the fight last night, I was standing alone, minding my own business when Hart came over to me. I guess he saw my Tennessee sweatshirt and figured I'd be sympathetic. He didn't say much, really. We got to talking about General Beauregard. I told him I was going to do a paper on the general. He seemed happy that I was going to write something nice about the man—"

Kincaid stopped talking abruptly. Finally Joe said, "Excuse me, Dennis, but what are you holding back?"

"I don't—I don't think he was serious."

"Who?" Joe demanded. "Hart?"

Kincaid nodded. Joe realized he was very upset.

"What did he tell you?"

Kincaid studied Joe in silence for a moment. There were tears in the corners of his eyes. "He said not to worry about Beauregard's reputation being sullied by that Yankee," he said. "That's what he called Professor Donnell. He said once the battle began, things would be taken care of."

When Frank and Joe ran up to the door of the library on the second floor, they saw that the sheriff was wrapping up the questioning of his last witness. The witness, a solemn middle-aged man in an ill-fitting Confederate uniform, was just nervously edging out the door. Joe stepped back to let the man pass, impatient to tell the sheriff what they'd found.

"I don't know, Joe," the sheriff said after the boys told him everything Kincaid had said. "I know you don't want to hear this, but I don't think all this amounts to much."

"But I was attacked on the stairs!" Joe reminded him.

"Yes, and we'll have to look into that," the sheriff admitted. "But one thing isn't necessarily connected to the other."

"Okay, suppose we agree with you that the attack on Joe isn't related to the professor's death," Frank offered. "That still doesn't explain why you don't think what Wesley Hart said to Kincaid is important."

The sheriff's tired face grew suddenly animated. "Fact is," he said angrily, "I'm the sheriff here, and I don't really have to explain anything to you two."

Joe stepped forward, eager to object, but the sheriff held up a hand to calm him. "I've known Wesley Hart all his life," he said wearily. "He's been a hothead ever since he was a boy, and he'll always be a hothead. He blows off steam, and then it's over. Far as I know, he never hurt a fly."

"There's a first time for everything, Sheriff," said Frank.

The sheriff agreed. "Of course there is. Look, I'll go ahead and talk to Wesley again myself. But don't you boys get your hopes up. And don't go getting involved, either. I'm telling you, Wesley is not our man."

Having said that, the sheriff stood up and announced, "I have not left this room in I don't know how long, and I intend to find myself something to eat. You're welcome to join me if you'd like."

"No thanks, Sheriff," Frank said to Joe's surprise. "But I did just think of something we could do for you. Has anyone checked the ammunition supply room downstairs, where the blanks came from?"

"Sure. My deputies went over it this afternoon and found nothing," answered the sheriff.

"Oh." Frank hesitated. "Well, you think we could have a peek at it?"

The sheriff hesitated. Joe could tell he didn't want to involve the Hardys any more than he had already. On the other hand, Joe knew, there was no real reason to bar them from a room that had already been searched by the police.

"Oh, okay," the sheriff said at last, taking a key out of his pocket. "Here. Tyler Pardee gave me this passkey. Go ahead, if you want to try your luck."

"Thanks," said Frank. "We will."

"Wow," said Joe as he followed his older brother into the dark, windowless ammunition room in the basement. He could tell that the room was fairly large, even before Frank flicked on the light. Once the light was on, Joe saw two rows of eight-foot-high metal shelves running down the center of the room. They were stacked high with boxes of blank cartridges.

"What are we looking for?" Joe asked his brother.

"Your guess is as good as mine," Frank said. "I thought if we found some live ammunition—but I don't know, maybe it'll be a waste of time."

Joe shrugged. "Well, we can try," he said. "I'll start here. You take that side."

Minutes passed as the brothers searched the boxes on the shelves. "Anything?" Joe asked.

"Not so far. Keep looking."

More minutes passed. Joe was about to suggest that they give up when he reached inside one more box of blanks and removed some bullets.

"I don't believe it," he said.

"Believe what?"

As Joe started to walk to Frank, Joe heard the door open behind him, and then the room went black—pitch-black.

Someone had come in and switched off the lights!

Chapter

6

"FRANK! YOU OKAY?"

"Yeah—shh." There was silence.

Frank knew that someone else was in the room. He strained his ears to hear any unusual sound and cautiously took a few steps forward, his hands out in front of him. Nothing. He took a few more steps and felt something brush against his shoulder. Just then an entire row of shelves toppled forward onto him, pinning him to the floor.

"Aaaaah!" he screamed.

"Frank," Joe cried.

The door flew open, and Joe caught a glimpse of a figure silhouetted for an instant against the light. Then it disappeared as the door was pulled closed.

"Frank!" Joe called again.

"I'm okay," Frank assured him, wondering if he was telling the truth. Just then the room was flooded with light. Joe had found the switch.

As Joe was digging his brother out of the rubble of shelves and ammunition, the door opened again and the sheriff appeared in the doorway, a chicken drumstick in one hand. Tyler Pardee stood beside him, and behind them was a small crowd of onlookers obviously drawn by the sudden noise.

Frank got to his feet cautiously, testing himself for broken bones. He grinned sheepishly at the crowd, noticing that Wesley Hart, Robert Merriweather, and Dennis Kincaid were among the onlookers.

"What on earth—" the sheriff said.

"I can explain, sir." Frank hobbled toward the men and, after the crowd had been dispersed, explained to him what had happened.

"Did you get a look at whoever did this?" Tyler Pardee asked when Frank had finished.

"Just a silhouette," Joe said. "I think it was a man." He glanced at his brother. "I have something else to tell you, Sheriff. Before the lights went out, I found this."

He handed a box of ammunition to the sheriff. "Take a look inside."

As the sheriff lifted out the shells, his eyes widened. "Well, I'll be."

"What is it?" Tyler Pardee and Frank asked.

The sheriff held up one of the shells. Unlike the flat-topped blanks, Frank observed that this one carried a hollow-nosed slug. "These are real bullets. This just might explain the shooting. It was an accident—a horrible accident, but not murder. I reckon the professor's family will have a beautiful lawsuit against the ammunition company, but it looks to me like you've wrapped up the investigation. Good work, boys."

Joe was surprised. "Hold on a minute, Sheriff. There are still a few questions that need answering."

"Such as?"

"For starters, who attacked me on the stairs? And who turned out the lights in the ammo room?"

The sheriff was not impressed. "When you've been in law enforcement as long as I have, son, you learn that it's rare when you can tie up every single loose end. I can't say why those other things happened, but I can say how the professor was probably shot. And that's what my report will state. His death was an accident."

"Does that mean we can go ahead with the reenactment tomorrow morning?" Pardee asked, shuffling his feet.

"I don't see why not," the sheriff answered. "I'll assign some men to go through the soldiers' ammunition and the shells in this room to make sure there aren't any more boxes like this one."

The sheriff paused and seemed very pleased.

"Well then, Tyler, that's that. Now I think I'm going to sample some of the Magnolia House's famous pecan pie."

Pardee threw an arm around the sheriff's shoulders. "Sheriff Walker, I'll not only join you, I'll treat."

He turned to the Hardys. "You boys care to come along?"

"No, thanks," Frank said absently before Joe could speak. Joe glanced at his brother, who seemed to be lost in thought.

"Suit yourself," said Pardee, and he and the sheriff left.

"What are you thinking?" Joe asked his brother as they straightened up the shelves.

"I'm thinking that there's more to this case than either Sheriff Walker or Tyler Pardee will admit. And I'm wondering why they both were so quick to say it's been solved."

Joe started to answer, but just then he saw something that turned his concerned expression into a smile. Jennifer Pardee had just breezed into the room. When she saw Joe, she approached him with a big smile on her face.

"Joe Hardy, there you are," she said. "I've been looking all over for you."

"I'm sorry," Joe said simply.

The look on Jennifer's face told him she understood. "It's so horrible about the professor," she said softly. "Daddy and I knew him for such a long time. But I just met Sheriff Walker upstairs, and he told me it was an accident.''

"Yes, well—yeah," Joe said awkwardly, not wanting to talk about the case.

His answer left an awkward silence, made worse by the fact that Frank was still lost in thought and hadn't even greeted Jennifer. Then quite suddenly Frank's face lit up and became animated. "Of course," he said. "Why didn't I think of it sooner?"

"Think of what, big brother?" Joe asked.

As an answer, Frank began to hurry toward the stairs to the first floor. "I have to check something out."

"Wait a minute. I'll go with you."

"You're leaving again?" Jennifer cried, sounding a little frustrated.

"Don't bother," Frank said, already on the stairs and taking them two at a time. "Get something to eat. I'll see you in our room later."

"But what—" Joe started to say, but was interrupted by Jennifer taking hold of his arm.

"It's okay. Frank'll take care of it, whatever it is," she said. "Come on, Joe, how about some supper. Then I'll take you over to Rebel Park and show you the rides. There's a real crowd there tonight, and that's when it's most fun."

"But he—" Joe started to tell Jennifer that he couldn't let Frank take on the burden of the case by himself. But Jennifer didn't know there *was* a case, and Joe knew his brother wouldn't want him to tell her. Better not to involve more people than necessary, he decided.

Jennifer tugged on his arm. Joe looked down at her and relaxed. "Okay," he said. "Sure. To tell you the truth, Jennifer, I think I could eat everything in the Magnolia's kitchen."

Frank still had the sheriff's passkey in his pocket, and he meant to use it to get into the professor's room. But when he got there, the door was standing open. Frank peered inside and saw Robert Merriweather sitting glumly on the bed, leafing through a stack of papers.

Frank hadn't seen the professor's room before. Bookcases stacked with volumes and papers lined one wall. On the far wall, in front of a large window, stood an enormous wooden desk piled high with more books and notebooks.

"Am I disturbing you?" Frank asked quietly.

Merriweather took a long time answering. When he did it was with a sad, softspoken no.

The assistant cleared his throat, sat up straighter on the bed, and said, "I mean, not at all. Come in. I was just trying to organize the professor's papers."

"I didn't realize he had so much stuff here," said Frank, entering the room and peering around. A large fireplace made it seem more like a library than a bedroom.

"Amazing, isn't it?" agreed Merriweather. "The professor used this room off and on for about two years. He'd come here approximately every other month for a few days to research the book on Beauregard.''

"Have you found anything at all," Frank said as gently as he could, "that might suggest who'd want to harm the professor?"

Merriweather smiled wanly. "The question is, who *wouldn't* want to harm him. But, no, I haven't come up with any name in particular. Of course I just started looking through his things."

Merriweather picked up the papers he had been reading, then put them down again. "You know, I don't think my heart is in this tonight," he said.

"That makes sense," said Frank.

Merriweather stood up and sighed. "I think I'll call it a day."

He started for the door. "You coming?"

"I was wondering," Frank said, "if you'd mind if I hang around for a few minutes, see what I can come up with?"

Merriweather hesitated. "I don't know—"

"I won't disturb anything. I just figured it couldn't hurt—you know, before I go down to supper."

Merriweather's face seemed to drain of all its color. He waved a hand toward the professor's desk. "Fine," he said, moving through the doorway. "You're a detective, right? Just lock up after you go."

After Merriweather left, Frank ran his eyes

around the room, trying to decide where to begin his search. The stack of papers that Merriweather had left on the bed proved to be of no use in pointing to a killer.

"Maybe the sheriff's right," Frank said out loud. "Maybe it was just a freak accident."

Even though he felt discouraged, Frank was no quitter. He moved to the bookcases to begin a systematic search for any clue to the identity of the person who had decided to do Donnell in.

"And this is my latest ride. The new disco tilt-a-whirl."

Joe stood next to Jennifer, watching the speeding circular ride. Its exterior was painted with southern plantation scenes to help it fit in with the park's theme. But the ear-splitting music, screaming passengers, and teenage disk jockey kept it planted firmly in the present.

"Not bad," Joe shouted over the noise, just as fifty passengers raised their hands off the safety rail and screamed in unison.

Jennifer giggled. "How do you know? You haven't even tried it yet! Come on, this ride's on me."

She pulled him toward the entrance to the ride. Joe held back at first. He was wondering what Frank was up to and wished he'd gone to help him. He was also a little worried about the food he'd eaten less than half an hour earlier. Would he be able to take this ride? Just watching the passengers whirling up and down and around made him feel a little woozy.

"What are you, chicken?" Jennifer teased. Then she saw his uneasy expression. "I'm sorry. You're thinking of the professor again," she said as though she could read his mind. "You know, Daddy told him not to write a book about Beauregard. He said there were too many people down here who'd get angry to hear their hero called a coward."

Joe just stared at her. "I thought you said his death was an accident."

Jennifer's green eyes widened. "I did. I just mean, if he hadn't been killed that way, sooner or later something even worse might have happened to him."

Joe shook his head, trying to make sense of what she said. But Jennifer pulled him toward the tilt-a-whirl.

"Come on," she said. "The ride's about to start again. Let's see what Yankee men are made of!"

Frank wearily tugged at the last drawer of Professor Donnell's desk. *I guess I'll have to give up and accept that the professor's death was an accident after this drawer.*

For nearly two hours Frank had searched every corner of the professor's room, read through every bit of correspondence, turned each book upside down and riffled through its pages for any kind of clue. All he had to show for it was dust up his nose and red eyes from reading.

Most of the papers had been photocopies of court records, old letters, and military orders—nothing that would indicate the identity of the professor's killer. This was the last desk drawer, and Frank was exhausted. He pulled at the drawer again, but it was stuck in its frame. Frank thought about not bothering to unstick it but decided finally to yank one last time.

Now the drawer stood open—and there it was.

Frank picked up the letter, noticing that it was dated just two weeks earlier. Reading, he learned that the professor's great-great-grandfather, a Union soldier, had killed the letter writer's great-great-grandfather, a Confederate soldier at Shiloh. "Maybe, at the reenactment, we can even the score," the letter ended.

Frank peered excitedly at the signature. It read, "Wayne Robinson."

Chapter

7

I DON'T BELIEVE IT! Frank read the letter one
more time to make sure he hadn't misinterpreted
it. It seemed clear enough—Robinson was threatening to avenge his great-great-grandfather's death
at the reenactment.

Frank ran out of the room with the letter. I
just hope Robinson hasn't left Memphis, he
thought as he raced down the marble stairs in
search of the sheriff. The little man, he remembered, lived in Georgia, but surely he'd wait
until after the reenactment to go back home.

Frank hurried through the first-floor rooms,
searching for the sheriff. At last he found him,
still in the dining room, sipping coffee and chatting with Tyler Pardee.

Incredible. Frank shook his head in wonder as
he watched the sheriff guffaw at one of Pardee's

jokes. He really thinks the professor's death was accidental!

He stuffed the incriminating letter into the pocket of his jeans and approached the sheriff's table.

"Frank!" Tyler Pardee smiled at the detective. "Sit down, relax! Let me get you a piece of pie."

"No, thinks, sir. Uh, Sheriff, I was wondering if I could have a word with you."

"What about, Frank?" The sheriff seemed to have completely forgotten about the professor.

"It's—uh, private."

The sheriff's face flickered with annoyance, but he wiped his mouth with a napkin, balled it up, and set it down as he stood up. "Okay," he finally said. "How about this table over here?"

It wasn't as private as Frank would have liked, but he was in no position to argue. He followed the sheriff to the table, pulled out the letter, and handed it to him before he sat down. "I found this in Professor Donnell's room. I think you should take a look at it."

As the sheriff read the letter, his expression changed.

"Pardee," the sheriff called, looking up from the letter. "What room's Wayne Robinson staying in?"

"How should I know?" Pardee called back with a grin. "Go ask at the front desk. Why do you want to know, anyway?"

Frank stood up, angry that the sheriff had let Pardee in on his discovery. Professionals knew better than to let everyone in on all the information, but the sheriff didn't seem to care who knew about this letter.

Not meeting Frank's eyes, the sheriff stood up and sauntered out of the dining room. "We've got another suspect," he called over his shoulder to Pardee. "Seems Wayne Robinson wrote a threatening letter."

"Robinson?" Pardee laughed. "He's nothin' but a good ol' boy."

Joe staggered off the tilt-a-whirl with Jennifer right beside him.

"How'd you like it?" she asked, her eyes shining with excitement. "That's just about my favorite ride."

"Mmm. Yeah," Joe said, trying to focus his blue eyes. "Especially that part where it went backward real fast and the disk jockey made us let go of the safety bar."

"Want to do it again?" Jennifer asked eagerly.

"Uh, not right now. But thanks."

Joe ran a hand through his blond hair. He wondered where Frank was and what he was up to. He felt guilty, leaving his brother alone while he was out having fun. Well, maybe fun wasn't the exact word for his ride on the tilt-a-whirl.

"Hey, come with me," Jennifer said as she tugged on his arm and led him across a still undeveloped field behind the rides. "I'll show you my favorite part of the park."

She took him nearly a quarter of a mile away from the glittering midway, to a large corral standing in open meadow and filled with horses softly whinnying and nickering in the moonlight.

"See?" Jennifer leaned against the corral, gazing out at the beautiful horses. Joe leaned against the fence beside her, admiring the stallions and graceful mares.

"They're still wild, most of 'em," Jennifer explained, reaching out to pat a curious filly on the nose. "They're my dad's hobby. He breaks them himself. For a guy his age he's a terrific horseman."

Joe nodded, reaching out to pat the filly himself.

"We put on a horse show every day, to show folks what a Southern cavalry unit looked like. Daddy says if we'd had as many men as we had good horses, things might have turned out differently." She shrugged and gave a little laugh. "Anyway, I love coming out here and looking at them in the moonlight."

"Yeah. Me, too," said Joe.

He gave a big yawn, and they both laughed.

"Tired?" asked Jennifer.

"Me? Well—maybe."

Jennifer smiled teasingly. "Just one more ride?"

Joe's face fell. He remembered the way his

stomach had felt when he stepped off the last time.

But he managed to take a deep breath, put an arm around her shoulders, and say, "Sure."

Frank walked with the sheriff toward Wayne Robinson's door at the big hotel. "I appreciate your doing this," Frank offered, trying to make up for the sheriff's obvious reluctance. "Maybe it is a wild-goose chase, but I feel as if we ought to check out every lead."

The sheriff was a good deal less amiable this time, Frank noticed, than he'd been before. "Fine" was all he said. "We'll check it out. Then I'm going home."

Wayne Robinson had apparently gone to bed for the night. It took him a long time to answer the door. When he did, he had on a bathrobe and appeared confused.

"Can we come in?" the sheriff asked.

"Yeah. Sure."

He nodded sleepily to Frank as he, too, stepped into the room. Frank eyed Robinson curiously. Half a foot shorter than Frank, he sure didn't look like a killer. Still, Frank told himself, you never knew.

Without wasting time, the sheriff showed the letter to Robinson and explained why they had come. Robinson sat down in a chair and read the letter, his face growing increasingly red.

"Yeah, I almost forgot about this," he said.

"Happened a few weeks back. I'm a big Civil War buff, see. Read all of Andrew Donnell's books. Why, I was the one who came across this information that his great-great-grandaddy killed mine. I remember, now, finding their names in some old battle records and laughing about it."

He tossed the letter down on a low table and gazed steadily at the sheriff. "This letter was meant as a joke, because I thought the coincidence was funny. I don't like what Donnell was saying about Beauregard any more than the next Southerner, but I had no grudge against him personally. And I don't take the past seriously enough to use it as an excuse to kill a man."

He shook his head. "I guess, under the circumstances, my little joke doesn't look too funny."

The room became silent. As though it had just occurred to him, Robinson added, "I've got people who can testify to where I was when Donnell was gunned down. I was way over on the other side of the field."

The sheriff nodded. Then he turned to Frank. "Satisfied?" he asked sharply.

Frank nodded. "Thank you," he said to Wayne Robinson. "We had to check this out."

"Sure you did." Robinson, weary and sad, accompanied them to the door. "The professor deserves no less."

"The tunnel of love?" Joe stared at the gaudily painted ride at the end of the midway. He was relieved that it wasn't the tilt-a-whirl but uncertain why Jennifer had brought him there.

"Sure. Why not?" Jennifer giggled.

"But, look. The operators are already gone." The midway was practically deserted. "For that matter, where is everybody?" he asked.

"The place is closing, silly." Jennifer playfully slapped his arm. "That's the fun of operating this place, though. I can go on the rides as late as I want. Come on. I know how to run it."

Still skeptical, Joe followed Jennifer to the entrance, where she jumped behind the operator's podium, switched a toggle, and stepped back to watch the lights and music come to life.

"Get in," she ordered, pointing to the first rowboat in a line at the entrance to the dark tunnel. "You row. I ride."

Grinning, Joe obeyed.

Inside, the only sound was that of Joe's oars lapping against the water.

"Don't go so fast," Jennifer teased him. "It's not the Indy five hundred, you know."

Smiling in spite of himself, Joe let up on the oars and tried to relax. After all, he was in a deserted tunnel facing a beautiful red-haired girl. Why couldn't he just relax and enjoy the situation?

"Come here. Sit next to me and stop rowing for a bit," Jennifer suggested, patting the seat beside her.

He started to respond when suddenly, back

from the way they had come, came the clank of a metal door being slammed.

Joe grabbed the oars again.

"What was that?" he yelled, glancing wildly down the dark tunnel.

Jennifer was also trying to locate the source of the noise. "Maybe the operator came back. It's Louie. He's always forgetting something."

"Why would he shut that entrance? That's what it sounded like, didn't it?"

Before Jennifer could answer, they heard a deafening roar from inside the tunnel. Joe spun around to see a pair of bright lights speeding toward them.

"Watch out!" Jennifer screamed. "It's a motorboat! It's going to hit us!"

Chapter

8

"DO SOMETHING!" Jennifer cried.

Joe stared at the headlights coming straight at them. The roar of the outboard motor was deafening.

"Is that where the exit is?" he yelled, pointing at the motorboat.

"Yes! It's behind that boat! There's no time! Joe!" Jennifer screamed.

"Jump!" he yelled, pushing Jennifer out of the boat into four feet of water.

Joe jumped and held Jennifer next to him flat against the tunnel wall. The motorboat plowed straight for the rowboat, sending it flying backward a few feet before splintering it into firewood. Then it roared off back through the tunnel, where the engine was cut off and footsteps could be heard running away.

"Joe?"

Jennifer's voice sounded tentative and scared. "You okay?" Joe asked her.

"Yeah. You?"

Joe pulled her close. "Yeah," he said. "Let's get out of here. Whoever was driving that boat might still be around."

Trembling and shivering in the chilly water, Jennifer led Joe through the tunnel to a service entrance. There they found the motorboat, its outboard motor still warm, bobbing in the gentle wake. Clearly, their attackers had used this boat and then run off.

"Who'd want to hurt us?" she asked. "I don't have any enemies."

Joe gave her a quick hug to console her. "Maybe you hang out with the wrong sort of guys," he commented dryly. "Obviously, somebody doesn't like the way my brother and I have been snooping around. We didn't want to tell you before, but Frank and I still believe the professor was murdered. And obviously, there is a killer, or we wouldn't have been attacked."

"I don't know about that." Jennifer sniffed, and then wiped her eyes. "Let's go back to the hotel," she said. "I've had enough excitement for tonight."

"What happened to you?" Frank sat up in bed, rubbed his eyes, and watched Joe pull off his water-soaked clothes.

70

"A little midnight swim," Joe joked, and then told his brother what had happened.

"Did you report it to the sheriff?"

"We told Jennifer's father, and he called the sheriff," Joe answered. "Mr. Pardee was very upset."

"That's understandable," said Frank.

"Yeah, but—"

"But what?"

"But—well, it seemed like he was madder at me for getting her in this situation than at the attackers. You know what I mean?"

Frank sighed and fell back against the pillows. "Yeah," he admitted. "I do know what you mean—people's priorities seem to be all mixed up. I mean, you don't see anyone weeping over the professor's death, do you? Most people are worried only about whether it's going to mess up the battle tomorrow."

Joe climbed into bed. "So, any news?"

Frank told him about the letter from Robinson. Near the end of the story, though, his words started to blur together and sleep threatened to take over.

"One thing's certain," Frank mumbled as he fell asleep. "Tomorrow we fight on the same side—and we stick as close together as we can."

It was still dark when Joe, in his Union uniform, and Frank, now in a blue uniform of his own, gathered with the troops on the rolling hills of Shiloh.

"What's the plan for this morning?" asked Joe, blowing on his fingers to warm them. It was extremely chilly in that predawn dark.

"We're supposed to attack the Southern camp at dawn," explained Frank, who had read up on the battle. "And whatever happens, we stay as close together as we can."

Joe nodded and yawned.

Frank studied his brother closely. "You don't look too good," he said.

"Two nights without my usual eight hours of beauty sleep," Joe joked. "I'll be okay, though."

Frank started to answer, but he was distracted just then by the appearance of Robert Merriweather astride a large black horse. "Look who's the new commander," Frank said, nodding toward Merriweather.

"That's weird," Joe remarked. "Why him?"

"I guess Pardee didn't want to do it today," Frank murmured. "I don't think Merriweather wanted to, either, but obviously he had no choice."

"Attention!" Merriweather called, trying to appear as commanding as possible in spite of his bulky appearance on the horse. "We'll be moving out soon, and I want you to keep it very quiet." He hesitated, as though trying to remember what he was supposed to say.

"I've chosen a second in command," he

added. "Dennis Kincaid, whom I believe many of you know."

A murmur ran through the troops as Kincaid rode up on another large black horse and saluted the soldiers. He looked very pale and very young, but he gave a perfect salute.

Frank saw the sun appear over the horizon behind the two men. "Get ready, everyone," Merriweather called. "We move out in four minutes."

Checking his gun to make sure it was loaded—and with blanks—Joe said, "I didn't know Merriweather knew Kincaid. He wasn't there yet when we met Kincaid in the airport, was he?"

Frank shook his head. "Just what I was thinking, but they could have met later." He and Joe joined the others in forming a long front line.

As they stood gazing at the Confederate camp, Merriweather rode in front of the troops, raised his right arm, and shouted, "Charge!"

The line, with Frank and Joe among them, moved as one across the fields of Shiloh in the dim light of dawn.

As he marched, Frank went over in his mind what he knew about the battle. The Southern camp was scarcely two hundred feet away, but the historical records claimed that the Confederates did not expect an attack and were caught completely off guard.

This time, though, the Confederates waited in front of their tents only until they heard Merriweather's yell. Then, unwilling to play the part of losers, they sounded their alarm immediately. In seconds Frank and Joe faced a battlefield ablaze with gunfire.

"Watch out!" Frank yelled to his brother as round after round of blanks were exchanged. Despite the noise and confusion, a big smile appeared on his face. As long as nobody got hurt, he realized, playing war could be fun—at least until exhaustion set in.

The Union troops were already using their cannons and had almost surrounded the Confederates, who were led that day by Tyler Pardee. That was why Merriweather was the Union commander, Pardee had obviously wanted to change sides and lead the South. Frank saw Pardee suddenly rear up on his horse and yell for a countercharge.

While Frank watched, the confederates responded with shouts and unintelligible yells. Joe grabbed his arm and pointed toward Merriweather, who was signaling a retreat.

As the Northerners pulled back toward the river, Frank yelled to his brother, "Stay close!"

"I'm with you!" Joe shouted, but with all the noise Frank could barely hear him.

Suddenly the Southerners decided to advance, and charged the retreating Union troops. The blue-uniformed soldiers took off, and Frank and Joe found themselves being pushed and tossed to the side of the battle. Troops rushed past them as they staggered backward into the brush.

"Come on!" Frank called to Joe. "We'll go around this way and avoid the crowds!"

Frank led the way through some thick underbrush. He could hear the battle to their left, but he couldn't see it. Finally he stopped and wiped the sweat from his face.

"Are you sure you know where we're going?" Joe demanded, coming up beside him.

"All I know is, we're somewhere in Tennessee," Frank admitted. The battle sounds were much fainter now. He decided it would be a good idea to take a short rest, then hike back through the clinging brush to rejoin their troops.

But before he could tell Joe his plan, he heard a new and unfamiliar sound.

"What's that?" he said, even as the realization began to dawn on his face.

"Horses!" Joe screamed. "A lot of them! Run!"

There was no time to run. A herd of horses was stampeding directly at the Hardys.

Frantically, Frank high-stepped through the thorn bushes that pulled at his legs and ankles. Behind him, Joe screamed to hurry. The noise of galloping horses thundered closer. There were no trees close enough that were big enough for the boys to climb.

"Too late!" he heard Joe yell.

It was later than Joe thought. Frank took one

last, desperate leap through the bushes, his brother close behind.

"W-what—" Frank stammered. But there wasn't time even to ask the question. The two brothers were falling through space.

They'd run off the edge of a high embankment and were falling toward the roaring Tennessee River!

Chapter

9

"AAARGHH!" the Hardys yelled as they hit the rocky slope, half rolling and half tumbling down toward the swirling waters below.

It was impossible for Joe to control his fall down the steep, gravelly bluff.

He did see his brother splash into the water. An instant later he, too, felt the shock of the cold current as he plunged in.

Joe worked hard to keep his head above the surface, but the current kept pulling him down. He looked for Frank but couldn't see him in the churning waves.

Joe pulled with his powerful arms to bring himself to the surface. But just as he was within inches, a powerful swirling eddy caught at him, forcing him to the bottom and pushing him downstream. Joe fought hard as his lungs quickly ran out of air. Frank, he thought weakly. But his brother wasn't there, no one was, and the weight of Joe's uniform was dragging him down, drowning him.

Suddenly he was tossed out of the churning spiral of water. Joe was free and shot to the surface, where he gasped in lungfuls of cool fresh air.

"Joe!" he heard Frank call out.

Sailing feetfirst, downstream on the current, Joe turned to see Frank near the bank of the river. He was caught up on a branch and was frantically trying to pull himself free. Branches tore at his arms, and his head was being repeatedly dunked beneath the surface of the water.

"Break the branch!" Joe yelled, speeding past.

"What?" Frank heard only the word *branch*, but the logic of the situation finally occurred to him. "Of course," he muttered to himself, attacking the branch. "Why didn't I think of that?"

On the fourth or fifth yank, the branch finally gave way and snapped in two, and Frank went sailing down the river in Joe's path, feetfirst in case of a collision with boulders.

Moments later he was treading water in quiet water downstream. Not fifty feet away, Joe was clinging calmly to a half-submerged log.

"Fancy meeting you here," Joe said with a weak grin.

Frank grinned back. "Let's get out of here."

Slowly, Joe led the way up the riverbank. At last, the brothers fell onto their backs on the grass, letting the morning sun warm them.

"That was close," Joe said after a while.

"Too close," Frank agreed. "Where'd those horses come from, anyway?"

"They could have been the same ones I saw last night, near Rebel Park," Joe mused. "Jennifer showed them to me."

Frank frowned. "You think there's any way this was an accident?"

"Who knows?" With an effort, Joe stood up. "I guess we should get back and find the real answers."

When the brothers rejoined the troops, Joe was surprised to see that the reenactment had been halted for a coffee break. Apparently, Pardee had made a few changes in the original battle plan.

When Robert Merriweather glanced up and spotted the Hardys, his eyes widened in surprise.

"You're—you're—" Merriweather sputtered. He paused and swallowed hard. "Where have you been? We were going to send a search party out for you."

"You're soaking wet," one of the other soldiers said. "What happened?"

Joe kept his eyes on Merriweather. "We were nearly killed by stampeding horses," Joe said. "Didn't any of you see them?"

"Sure we did," snapped Merriweather. "But we didn't know you were in their path. You fell into the river?"

Ignoring his question, Frank said, "How did the horses get out of their corral?"

"How should I know?" answered Merriweather. "You must be hungry. Grab a danish or doughnut and sit."

Joe decided not to argue with that. He walked over to a table loaded with pastries and coffee. Frank hung back to ask Merriweather, "Where's Kincaid?"

"I didn't see him all morning until I caught a glimpse of him going off with everyone else on horseback to round up the horses. That's why the reenactment stopped. Everyone was trying to halt the stampede."

"Except you," Joe pointed out, rejoining them with a plateful of doughnuts.

Merriweather scowled. "I'm not a good rider," he said.

"How about Kincaid?"

"He is an excellent horseman," Merriweather answered.

"There he is now." Joe nodded at a horse galloping toward them. Kincaid dismounted near the Hardys, announcing to the group in his southern accent, "Now, *that* was really something."

"The stampede?" Joe asked.

Kincaid nodded. "Never seen anything like it in my life."

"Is everything under control now?" Merriweather asked.

Joe glanced at the graduate assistant. He sounded awfully nervous.

Kincaid gave Merriweather a significant look, "There's nothing to worry about."

"Where were you when the stampede started?" Frank asked Kincaid.

"With Robert, of course," Kincaid said. "I led the retreat with him."

"But I thought—" Joe started to say. Then he saw Frank signal silence and shut his mouth.

"Joe, can I talk to you for a minute?" Frank asked.

"Sure." Joe followed his brother a short distance away.

"What's going on?" Joe asked Frank as soon as they were out of hearing distance of the other people. "Kincaid's story didn't jibe with Merriweather's."

Frank nodded. "I know. Merriweather denied having seen Kincaid since the battle started, yet they were supposed to have led the retreat together. What really gets me, though, is that I didn't know these guys even knew each other, and they're acting like accomplices."

"I don't know, Frank. Let's forget it and just

get through the rest of the reenactment, okay? After that, we can work full-time on the case."

Frank nodded as Joe heard someone clearing his throat behind him. He spun around.

"Oh. Excuse me." The pasty-faced Martin Crowley jumped back, startled by Joe's sudden movement. "Am I interrupting something?"

"No, Mr. Crowley," Frank said. "What can we do for you?"

Crowley approached the boys again, cautiously. His Union uniform looked awkward on his round-shouldered frame, as though it was a size too big for him. As he approached, he kept glancing over his shoulder at the other soldiers drinking coffee nearby. Joe realized, suddenly, that the little man was very much afraid of something.

"I don't know where to begin exactly," Crowley said in a near-whisper.

"Does it have to do with Professor Donnell?" Joe asked.

"Well, yes and no—" Crowley hesitated. "I guess it's better to just tell you."

"Tell us what?" demanded Frank.

"Well, you see, it's this way. Oh, this is rather embarrassing."

"What?" Joe asked impatiently.

But before Crowley could answer, Dennis Kincaid, back on his horse, rode up to them. Joe couldn't help but notice the look he was directing at Crowley, who trembled visibly. Why is Crowley afraid of Kincaid? Joe wondered.

"Gentlemen, the break is over," Kincaid drawled. "Time to resume battle formation. Move out."

With a last look at Crowley, Kincaid rode away.

"Well," Joe said, turning back to the little man. But Crowley was gone. Joe turned to find him trying to slip away.

"Hey, wait a minute!" Joe started after him, followed by Frank. "What'd you want to tell us?"

"Oh, nothing, nothing!" Crowley called out as he walked quickly away from the brothers. "It was nothing, really. I changed my mind. I'll tell you later."

"When?" Frank called after him, frustrated.

"After the battle. At Magnolia House."

The afternoon's reenactment was as loud and chaotic as the rest of the morning's, Joe decided as he aimed his rifle at the now familiar-looking Confederate soldiers. "I know I already shot that guy," he said out loud to himself as he popped another blank into an enemy soldier's shoulder. The Confederate cried out convincingly and fell to the ground, supposedly wounded, but Joe knew that the minute he turned his back, the soldier would get back on his feet and start shooting.

In any case the enthusiastic crowd of onlookers kept everyone fighting energetically. Whenever Joe "killed" an enemy soldier, he could count on a round of applause, just audible over the noise of gunfire. In fact, he began to really enjoy playing for the audience—braving enemy fire and attempting foolhardy exploits to see how many people he could get to cheer him on.

It came as a nasty surprise, then, when the gunfire abruptly stopped, right in the middle of the battle.

Joe turned to Frank, who'd stuck close to him all afternoon.

"What's going on?" Joe asked.

Frank didn't have time to answer. From the far side of the battlefield, Joe heard a cry.

"He's dead!" the voice was screaming. "He's dead!"

"What?" Joe exchanged a quick glance with Frank, and the two brothers began running toward the source of the uproar. As he drew closer, Joe could see a crowd gathered. Joe pushed his way through the crowd.

In the center of a circle of soldiers, flat on his back, lay Martin Crowley, his eyes closed, his mouth half open, and a widening circle of dark red blood staining the front of his Union blues.

Chapter

10

"Oh, no." Frank stared at Crowley's still body. He'd been shot in the chest, just like Professor Donnell.

"I can't believe it happened again," he heard Joe say, while feeling for a pulse in Crowley's limp, white wrist.

Frank heard the moan of a siren in the distance. Too late to help Crowley, Frank knew. The arrival of the paramedics took away all pretense that this was 1862 and that this death was anything but real.

Frank backed away from the scene just as Tyler Pardee rode up. "What happened here?" Pardee demanded.

"Another shooting," Frank explained. "Martin Crowley's been murdered."

"Crowley?" Pardee's expression was stunned. As Frank watched, the hotel owner dismounted and joined the crowd of onlookers.

Better late than never, Frank thought, exchanging a glance with his brother. He listened to the muttering crowd, realizing that there was a feeling of real fear in the air now. He knew that all of Crowley's acquaintances were wondering, How was he killed? Why was it Crowley? And who would be next?

"All right, I admit it," the sheriff was saying to the Hardys as they stood before him in the library at Magnolia House. "I probably should have listened to you boys earlier. Not that I'm entirely convinced about the professor, mind you. But I just don't see how poor old Martin Crowley's death could have been an accident."

Frank watched the sheriff shake his head in bewilderment. You ought to be sorry, he thought angrily. If it wasn't for your stubbornness, Crowley might still be alive. But Frank knew his anger contained plenty of guilt. Hadn't Crowley tried to tell them something earlier? And hadn't it been the Hardys who had let him walk off, unprotected?

"Let's figure out what we should do now," Frank suggested. "Do you think Joe and I should work on finding a connection between the professor and Crowley while you and your men question any witnesses?"

The sheriff leaned back in his leather chair and nodded. "Sure," he said in a low voice. "Sounds okay to me. But meet me back here in, say, three hours, to check in."

Frank stared out the window at the magnolia-strewn lawn and let out a deep, thoughtful sigh.

"It's a tough one, huh?" he heard his brother say sympathetically.

"You can say that again." Frank took a sip of soda from a glass.

"I mean, it's not as if either the professor or Crowley was the most likeable guy in the world," Joe went on.

"That's for sure," agreed Frank.

"But who'd want to kill them? And what I want to know," Joe said, "is why Merriweather acted so nervous today."

"Right," said Frank. "And how come he and Dennis Kincaid are so chummy?"

"Exactly." Joe stood up from his chair in the dining room, where they'd headed to talk after leaving the sheriff. "We've got our work cut out for us, brother."

"Where do you want to start?"

"Let's go back to the professor's room. I know you've searched it already, but maybe a second set of eyes will turn up something new."

This was Joe's first time in the professor's room, and he was suitably impressed. "Wow," he said after walking inside behind Frank, who had unlocked the door with the passkey. "Some roadside inn."

"Yeah. Whatever else you say about the professor, he sure knew how to live," Frank remarked. "Seems kind of weird, though, being in here after he's gone. Where do you want to start looking?"

Joe thought for a moment. "Why don't you check the closet and chest of drawers. I'll go through the desk," he said. "If we can't find a tie between the professor and Crowley maybe something else will turn up to answer some of our questions."

They searched in silence for a few minutes—Joe working his way through the desk drawers while Frank moved from the chest of drawers to the closet. He started searching through the professor's jacket pockets.

Joe glanced over in time to see Frank pull a piece of paper out of one of the pockets.

"Find anything?" he asked.

"Yeah," he said. "A dry cleaner's receipt from Bayport."

Joe turned back to the desk as Frank continued pulling papers out of the professor's raincoat, trousers, and sports coat. "Most of these are notes the professor made to himself," Joe heard him say. "Things about his book. Here's one about travel arrangements."

A moment later Frank remarked, "You know, he was pretty organized. He put the date on every note. Sometimes he even numbered notes consecutively by subject. Pretty amazing.''

Joe paused for a long time as he read something interesting he had pulled from the desk.

"Oh, yeah?" he said at last. "Then come look at this."

Joe showed the note he'd found to his brother. "See? A corner's been torn off. Is that where he usually puts the date?"

"Let me see—" Frank read the note.

Robert,
   Contact the County Clerk's office at Shiloh to determine who owns the property surrounding the National Park.

Frank looked up, smiling broadly.

"Crowley was the county clerk," he remembered. "Joe, I think you may have found something."

Robert Merriweather was even more nervous now than before, Joe realized as he and Frank interrogated him about the professor's note.

Merriweather sat on the bed in his room, sipping a cup of tea. Joe noticed that Merriweather's hands shook each time he lifted the cup to his lips. With each sip, he spilled some of the tea and nervously replaced the cup on the nightstand. Then, seconds later, he would look at the tea cup and start the whole process over again.

"Robert." Frank's voice sounded amazingly patient. "Why are you so nervous?"

"Why shouldn't I be?" The chubby man looked from one brother to the other. "The professor's been murdered, and now Crowley's dead. I'm terrified."

"You've been nervous ever since we got to Memphis," Joe pointed out.

"I've been under a lot of pressure. Professor Donnell wasn't an easy person to work for."

"All right," Frank said. "Never mind about that now. Just tell us what you can about this note."

Merriweather studied the note Joe handed him. "I never saw it," he finally announced. "He never gave it to me."

"Any idea why it wouldn't have a date on it?" asked Joe. "Or do you think someone tore it off on purpose?"

Joe tried to be patient as Merriweather picked up his teacup, then set it down again. "I haven't the slightest idea," he said at last.

"You don't know who owns the land around the national park?" asked Frank.

"Pardee, I assume. We're on that land." Merriweather laughed weakly.

"Fine," Joe interrupted. "Now tell us this. How long have you known Dennis Kincaid."

Merriweather's eyes widened slightly. "As

long as you, I guess. Just met him two days ago.''

Joe started to protest, but Merriweather's face had suddenly taken on a set, determined look.

"I'm exhausted," he said, picking up his teacup and, hands steady, he took a big drink of the hot liquid. "I don't want to answer any more questions right now."

"Fine," Frank said. He started for the door. Joe hesitated but then changed his mind, remembering how stubborn the assistant could be. Reluctantly he followed his brother out of the room.

"What did all that mean?" he asked Frank as the two of them strode down the corridor.

"I think it means we're onto something," said Frank in a low voice. "But first I think we should check in with the sheriff. It's nearly time."

As he spoke, Joe was passing the professor's room, where they'd found the incriminating note earlier. Joe glanced at it, then stopped dead in his tracks.

"I thought you locked the door," he said to his brother.

"I did—" Frank glanced toward the room and he, too, stopped cold.

The door to the professor's room was wide open.

Chapter

11

SILENTLY FRANK MOTIONED for Joe to move to the far side of the doorway.

Once they were in position on either side of the door, Frank raised a hand as a signal to enter. As he brought the hand down he yelled, "Now!"

The Hardys burst into the room to find Dennis Kincaid standing near the desk. When he saw the brothers, he froze.

"Get him!" Frank yelled, leaping for him.

But Joe had already made a flying tackle on Kincaid, crashing with him onto the bed.

Frank relaxed. Very few people could wriggle out of one of Joe's football tackles, particularly not an underweight college kid. But to his surprise, Kincaid refused to stop fighting. He struggled against Joe for several seconds, hitting him hard in the stomach before knocking the breath out of him, and sliding off the bed and onto the floor.

"What's going on?" Kincaid gasped as Frank stepped up to him.

"You tell us!" Joe demanded.

Kincaid said nothing but only fought to control his breathing.

"How did you get in here?" Frank asked.

Kincaid glared at the older Hardy but still said nothing.

"Fine," Frank said, his blood boiling. "You can tell it to the sheriff, then. He's always interested to hear from someone who's into breaking and entering."

"I didn't break in," Kincaid snarled. "The door was open."

"It was—" Joe started to say, but Frank stopped him.

"What were you looking for?" asked Frank.

Kincaid's mouth turned down stubbornly. Suddenly he flared out, "I just wanted a souvenir of the professor!"

"And you were just going to take something?" asked Joe.

"I would've okayed it with Merriweather," Kincaid answered, trying to sound annoyed.

"Did you find anything?" Frank asked in a steely voice.

93

"No." Kincaid paused. He seemed to be deflated. "No. I didn't find anything."

"Get out of here," Joe growled.

Kincaid struggled to his feet and pushed his pale hair out of his eyes. "I think I will."

After he left the brothers exchanged a quick glance. Frank shrugged. "Let's go find the sheriff," he said, and took out the passkey to lock the door behind them.

"It isn't just the fact that these murders could kill my business—so to speak," Tyler Pardee was shouting as Frank and Joe approached the upstairs library. "But my own daughter's under attack, Sheriff. I'm telling you, Walker, this is not going to look good for you come election time."

"Excuse me?" Frank knocked on the half-open door. "Can we come in?"

Pardee motioned for the Hardys to enter without stopping his tirade. "What have you and your men found so far?" he demanded of the miserable sheriff.

"We know Crowley was shot with the same kind of bullet as Professor Donnell, and from a distance," the sheriff recited in a monotone. He turned to Frank and Joe with dim hope lighting his downcast face. "You boys find anything?"

Frank snapped his head toward Joe, "Let me do the talking." Then he addressed the sheriff.

"Not much, I'm afraid," he said. "But I did have some questions for Mr. Pardee."

"For me?" Tyler Pardee seemed very surprised.

"Only a few, actually," said Frank.

"Shoot."

Frank took the passkey out of his pocket. "I got this from the sheriff. How many more of these are there?"

"Just one other," Pardee said.

"Who has the other one?" Frank asked.

"I do."

"May I see it?" asked Frank.

Frank smiled to himself as Pardee grimaced in exaggerated annoyance. But the middle-aged hotel owner dragged the other passkey out of a trouser pocket and held it up for Frank to see.

"Thanks," Frank said. "Oh, and one other thing. Who owns the property around the national park?"

Pardee's face turned to stone.

"What's this all about?" he demanded.

"Just curious," Frank said mildly. "But I think it might have something to do with the murders."

"Can't imagine why you'd think that. Anyway, all that land's been in my family since before the real Battle of Shiloh."

"The deeds are on file at the courthouse?" Frank persisted.

"Sure," Pardee snapped. "Now you tell me

something. What's my land got to do with two men getting shot and my daughter almost getting mowed down by a motorboat?"

"Good question." Frank moved away. "Unfortunately, I don't have an answer yet."

The sheriff's face turned red. "If you boys are onto something you'd better tell me right now," he said. "There's a killer on the loose, and I wouldn't be at all surprised if he went after you two next."

"Don't worry, sir," Frank said, moving toward the door with Joe following. "If we figure something out, you'll be the first to know."

"Now what?" Joe asked as they made their way toward the marble staircase.

"Search me," Frank said gloomily. "I was hoping something would shake loose from Pardee, but all I did was make him mad. I tell you, Joe, right now everyone looks suspicious around here." He glanced at his brother and was surprised to see a thoughtful expression on his face. "How about you?" he asked.

"I was thinking," Joe said slowly as they descended the stairs to the foyer. "Jennifer said something kind of funny last night, before we went on the rides."

"What's that?"

"She said her dad tried to talk the professor out of writing a book on General Beauregard.

Now, why would he want to do that? Seems a book could only help his business.''

Frank frowned. "Search me. Maybe he figured it would get folks down here too mad."

Joe thought it over. Then he said impulsively, "How about checking out Pardee's horses with me? They should be back in the corral by now. Something about that whole stampede doesn't sit right with me."

Frank was surprised and shrugged. "Sure," he agreed, following Joe to the door. "How can it hurt?"

In the pink light of sunset Joe led Frank through the amusement park to the corral at the far end of the fields. The horses were peacefully grazing, as though they hadn't nearly caused the Hardys' death a few hours before.

"Hmm," Joe said, glancing at a stable and barn with construction equipment lined up against the side of it. "I don't remember seeing all that last night."

"You had eyes only for Jennifer," Frank teased.

Joe grinned. "It was dark," he said, "that's all." Then he nodded toward a spot where the corral had obviously been mended. "It looks like the horses got out through there."

"You got that right," said a voice behind the Hardys.

Frank and Joe were startled by a grizzled old man dressed in dusty cowboy clothes. White hair and a beard stuck out from under his battered hat, and his thin shoulders were hunched up beneath his red western shirt. "Name's Ben," he said. "I run the stable for Mr. Pardee. Can I help you boys?"

"We were wondering how the horses broke out this morning," Joe said.

Ben scratched his chin whiskers. "I figure it was all this new construction. Maybe the digging weakened the fences and somethin' spooked the horses and they bolted."

"Did you see it happen?" asked Frank.

The old cowboy shook his head. "I was in the barn spreadin' hay."

Joe asked, "Did you see a young, skinny, blond guy here around that time?"

"You mean Dennis?"

"You know him?" asked Joe.

"Oh, sure, he's been around a few times."

The Hardys said nothing.

"Can't say if he was here before the stampede," Ben continued. "But I do know he was here before the shooting. I remember 'cause the noise of the battle was still going on. After Crowley got shot, everything went quiet."

The Hardys thought this over while Ben rattled on, oblivious of whether or not they were listening. "Shame about Crowley. I always liked him. Even voted for him, and that could have cost me my job if anyone found out."

"Why's that?" asked Joe.

"You boys don't know much, do you? Crowley wasn't popular around here. Mr. Pardee was campaign manager for his opponent in the last election."

"Who was his opponent?" asked Frank.

"Wayne Robinson," said Ben.

"Wayne Robinson," Frank repeated incredulously. "He lives in Macon, Georgia."

"He does now, but until six months ago he lived right here in Memphis," said Ben. "Listen, I'd love to keep chatting with you boys, but they've got supper waiting for me at the house."

"Of course," said Frank. "Thanks for your help."

"You two take care around here," added Ben, walking away. "Plenty of construction pits to stumble into."

"So Dennis Kincaid was here before," Frank suggested after Ben had gone. "We'll ask him about it when we get back to the hotel. Anything else you want to check out while we're here?"

"The barn?" Joe said. He didn't think there'd be much to see, but all the construction equipment intrigued him. Besides, it was so peaceful away from a hotel full of terrified guests.

The Hardys walked slowly across the meadow to the barn in the evening light. It was painted rust red and had a peaked wooden roof. Tall metal scaffolding hugged the side nearest the boys like a metal shell.

Joe entered the barn first, followed by Frank.

Inside, it was spacious and very dark. Rays of light filtered in through the ill-fitting boards on the roof and landed in pale streaks on the hay-strewn floor.

"Wish we had some light," Joe heard Frank say behind him.

Joe found a switch and threw it, but nothing happened. "Power must be off because of the construction."

"Maybe we should come back in the morning," Frank suggested.

"Yeah, maybe so," said Joe. He heard something—or someone—move behind him in the dark.

"What was that?" he asked.

"What was what?"

Then they both heard a creaking sound.

"It sounds like—" Joe started to say. Then he stopped. No, it couldn't be. He looked up through the darkness toward the front wall, the one with the scaffolding. Was it shifting?

"The wall!" Frank shouted behind him. "It's collapsing!"

Chapter

12

"RUN!" YELLED JOE. He turned and raced toward a side entrance, grabbing Frank by the arm and yanking him outside just in time.

Behind them, an entire section of barn wall collapsed. Enormous clouds of dust blew out all around Frank and Joe.

"That was too close," Frank said, stunned.

Joe slapped dust from his clothes. "You can say that again. And we've had too many close calls since we got here." He and Frank stumbled, still slightly dazed, across to the corral, where the horses were snorting and pawing at the dust nervously, and sat down.

A few moments later Joe looked up to see Tyler Pardee, the sheriff, and Ben running toward them.

"What happened here?" demanded the sheriff.

"You tell us," said Joe."

"You boys okay?" Pardee seemed to be shaken, even in the dim evening light.

"We'll be okay after we clean up a bit," Joe said, still brushing dust and grit out of his hair and off his shirt. "Never dull around here, is it?" he said to Pardee.

"Thank goodness you weren't hurt," the hotel owner replied.

Ben said, "I told 'em to be careful around here. Last thing I said to 'em. Then I was sittin' in the kitchen eating supper and I heard that crash, and I just *knew* it had to be the barn—especially with the rides shut down for the night—"

"Fine, Ben," Mr. Pardee interrupted. "Why don't you round up some men and check out what caused the wall to collapse."

"Yes, sir, Mr. Pardee."

As the Hardys, Pardee, and the sheriff walked back toward Magnolia House, Frank said to the sheriff, "Sir, I was wondering if we could have another private talk with you. It won't take long."

"Doubtful, son," the sheriff said matter-of-factly.

"What do you mean?" asked Joe.

"It means he doesn't need any more private talks," Pardee said with obvious satisfaction. "The case is closed."

"What do you mean, closed?" said Frank.

"It's true," answered the sheriff. "We were looking to tell you fellas when we heard the barn wall collapse. We've arrested Wayne Robinson for the murders of Martin Crowley and Andrew Donnell."

The Hardys stared at him, stunned.

Frank was still going over what had happened the next morning as he and Joe ate breakfast in the dining room.

"It just doesn't add up," he said to his brother, who was digging into a heaping plate of buttermilk pancakes, sausages, and grits. "One minute Pardee's yelling at the sheriff to solve this case pronto, and the next minute he and the sheriff are all buddy-buddy, talking about how Robinson shot both Donnell and Crowley. I don't know. Maybe I'm wrong, but I smell a rat."

"A rat?" Joe turned to see Jennifer Pardee standing behind them, her hands on her hips. "You didn't see one around here, did you? How awful!"

"Not a real one." Joe pulled out a chair for Jennifer.

"Frank was just saying he doesn't think Wayne Robinson's responsible for those killings," Joe explained.

"Why not?"

"First of all," Frank answered, "Robinson has an airtight alibi for the professor's murder.

We talked to a crowd of people who were with Robinson on the far side of the field when it happened.''

Jennifer said, ''But Daddy told me he wrote a threatening letter to the professor, and he did hate Mr. Crowley. I don't think you boys understand southern politics. It can get ugly.''

''Ugly enough to lead to murder?'' asked Frank.

Jennifer shrugged, turning a little pink.

Joe added, ''I honestly don't think he'd do it at all after being suspected of shooting the professor.''

Jennifer frowned. ''You may be right. What are you going to do now, and how can I help?''

''For starters,'' said Frank, ''while Joe finishes his breakfast, I'll make a quick phone call. Then I want to look at the supply tent on the battlefield where they kept the extra ammo.''

''The place Wesley Hart was in charge of,'' Joe added.

''Right. I haven't ruled him out as a suspect yet,'' said Frank. He glanced at Jennifer, who was listening attentively. He didn't like discussing the case in front of her, but he sensed that she was really on their side.

''After that, I want to drive to the courthouse to check out some deeds.''

''Can I come along?'' asked Jennifer.

Frank looked from her to Joe, then back to

her. "We'll need you to show us the way to the courthouse," he said, relenting.

As Joe waited with Jennifer in the foyer of Magnolia House for Frank, he wished that for once he and Frank could have made it through an entire vacation without getting involved in a mystery. Here I am, he thought glumly, with one of the prettiest girls I've ever seen, and all I can think about are dead people. Oh, well. He shrugged. Better luck next time.

Joe's thoughts were interrupted by Frank. "So? What gives?" he asked his brother.

"A lot gives," Frank said with obvious satisfaction. "I just talked to the dean of men at Tennessee State University."

"Dennis Kincaid's school?" Joe interrupted.

"Yes and no," said Frank.

"What does that mean?" asked Jennifer.

"It means that that's where Kincaid says he goes to school, but there's no record that he was ever enrolled there."

Joe shook his head, impressed with his brother's detective work. "What tipped you off?"

"First of all he had a room at the hotel, which seemed very odd. Then Ben, down at the corral. He said he'd seen Dennis around there several times. But Dennis told the professor this was his first time at Magnolia House. Kincaid should have made sure his cover story held water."

"Why would he need a cover story?" asked Jennifer.

"That," said Frank, "is just one of the things I want to ask him. Let's all pay a visit to Dennis Kincaid's room."

This time Jennifer Pardee led the way to the upstairs room. Joe was amused at her determination to help the detectives, and he let her run ahead after he had told her the room number.

But when they knocked at Kincaid's door, there was no answer.

"Not really a surprise," Frank commented.

"What now?" Jennifer asked.

"We could try Merriweather's room," offered Joe. "The two of them seem to be pretty friendly lately."

"Good idea," said Frank.

But to Joe's disappointment, there was no answer at Merriweather's door, either.

"This isn't getting us anywhere," Joe said.

"Right," Frank agreed. "Let's check out the ammo tent as we'd planned, and we'll look for Kincaid later."

Frank was surprised at how calm and beautiful the battlefield appeared in the midmorning spring light. It was hard to believe it was the same place where Frank had watched hundreds of people in uniform firing rifles and cannons.

But sure enough, there in the middle of what

had been designated neutral territory for the reenactment, Frank spotted the ammo tent.

"Hurry up," he called to Joe and Jennifer, who lingered behind him. He started jogging toward the olive green canvas structure. Approaching the entrance, he saw that the tent was about twelve feet tall and perhaps thirty feet on each side.

Frank stepped inside and was once again confronted by shelves stacked with boxes of blank cartridges. He stood in the doorway for a while, trying to decide where to begin his search.

"Here we go again," he said aloud.

"Talking to yourself, big brother?" Joe teased as he and Jennifer entered the tent.

"You caught me."

Jennifer studied the shelves. "Dad should have had someone take this down by now," she commented. "What is it you're looking for?"

"Anything that doesn't look as if it belongs here," Frank replied.

"You'll know it when you see it," Joe explained.

Jennifer was skeptical. "If you say so."

Frank began searching the shelves on the far left of the tent, while Jennifer took the middle and Joe wandered off toward the right. After a few minutes' silence Joe said, "You know, there's an excellent chance we won't find anything."

"I know," Frank admitted, "but let's give it a little time."

It was hot in the tent, and even Frank thought about giving up after another fifteen minutes of fruitless searching. He paused to wipe his face on the tail of his shirt. Then he froze. He heard a very unsettling sound.

"What's that?" he said.

"What?" Jennifer wandered over to him.

"That hissing sound. Like steam leaking from a pipe."

Jennifer looked around. Then she started sniffing. "There's smoke."

Just then one shelf, then another, crashed to the ground behind them. Jennifer screamed as Joe came running toward them as fast as he could.

"Run for it!" he yelled at the top of his lungs. "The tent's on fire! It's going to explode!"

Chapter

13

"IT HASN'T REACHED the ammo yet, though," Frank snapped as the three ran for the entrance, climbing over the shelves Joe had accidentally knocked over.

"Not yet," yelled Joe. "But it could any minute, and when it docs it will blow this battlefield off the map."

Frank knew his brother was right. Blanks might not have slugs in them, but they did have gunpowder—and gunpowder explodes.

"Get her out of here," Frank said, pushing Jennifer toward his brother. "I'm going to try to put out the fire."

"What!" Joe was already shoving Jennifer through the entrance. "Forget it, Frank!"

"Nobody can stop this but us," Frank insisted,

looking around wildly for something to fight the fire with. In a corner he spotted a pile of army blankets and charged for them.

"I'll be right back," Joe yelled after him. Frustrated and angry with his brother for taking such a risk, he ran outside and yelled to Jennifer, "Run! We're going to try to put out the fire!"

"You're what?" Jennifer yelled.

"We're going to put it out!" Joe hoped he didn't look as foolish as he felt.

"Don't be stupid!" Joe heard the girl scream as he turned back toward the tent, but it was too late. He saw Frank at the far end of the space, beating at the canvas with a blanket. Instantly, Joe was at his brother's side.

"Fancy meeting you here," Frank joked, pounding at the flames. But the fire continued to grow, and as it did, the smoke grew thicker and blacker. Frank broke down in a fit of coughing.

"Give me those," Joe said brusquely, reaching for some of the blankets. He threw the blankets on the flames, smothering one area after another. But the fire continued to work its way closer to the shelves of ammo.

"Frank," he said. "We've got to get out of here."

Frank was coughing too hard to answer.

"Come on, Frank," Joe said, hustling Frank toward the entrance and up and over the fallen shelves.

He practically pulled his brother to the edge of

the open battlefield, where they caught up with Jennifer.

"Don't stop!" Joe yelled at her. "It'll blow any second!"

Jennifer took Frank's other arm, and the three of them made it to a small knoll a safe distance away.

KABOOOOOOOM!

The ammo tent erupted in a tremendous explosion that rocked the ground. Tiny bits of debris began to rain down on the trio even as far away as they were. But to Joe's relief, they were safe.

"Looks like we won't be turning up any evidence there," Joe said wryly.

Frank surveyed the remains of the tent. Where he, Joe, and Jennifer had been standing only moments before, there was now a black, smoldering hole in the earth.

Frank studied the field to see if he could spot anyone else, but he wasn't surprised that there was no one in sight. He pointed to a row of trees a couple of hundred feet from the tent. "Whoever set the fire probably ran in there," he said to the others.

"Someone purposely set that fire," Jennifer stated. "But why?"

"We're getting too close to the killer," said Frank, "and he knows it."

Frank spotted a group of workers from Rebel Park running toward them. Among them was old Ben from the corral.

"We heard the explosion," Ben said when he caught up with them on the edge of the blackened field. "We called the fire department. Are you okay, Miss Pardee?"

"We're fine." Jennifer was impatient to be moving. "Ben, would you do us a favor? Would you wait for the sheriff, and when he gets here, tell him that someone purposely set fire to that tent. We don't know who it was. We'd stay but we have to get down to the county courthouse."

"I'll tell the sheriff," Ben said, looking mystified.

"Good," said Jennifer. "Then we're on our way."

The boys started to protest, then shrugged and followed Jennifer to her car.

Fifteen minutes later the Hardys were speeding in Jennifer's red convertible along a Tennessee country road. Jennifer was driving. Joe sat next to her. Frank sat in the back seat, trying to put together the pieces of the case.

"Um, Frank?" Jennifer said, glancing at him in the rearview mirror. "Don't look now, but I think we're being followed."

Frank moved closer to the middle of the back seat and studied the road behind them in Jennifer's rearview mirror. A navy blue pickup truck was perhaps a quarter mile back down the road.

"That could be the truck that nearly ran over

us at the airport," said Joe, who had spotted the truck in the sideview mirror.

"That's what I was thinking," said Frank. "Do you recognize it, Jennifer?"

She raised her eyes to the rearview mirror again, then shook her head no. "There are an awful lot of pickup trucks in Tennessee."

Frank sighed. "Let's just keep an eye on it then," he said, "and see what happens."

A few miles later the blue pickup pulled off the road. The Hardys and Jennifer breathed easier.

When they arrived at the county courthouse, Frank was the first one out of the car. Jennifer and Joe followed him to the office of the recorder of deeds.

"Afternoon, Miss Pardee," said the woman behind the counter. She was a slender blond in her late fifties with what Frank thought might be a permanent scowl on her face.

"Afternoon, Miss Beaumont," Jennifer said. She explained what they were there for, and the woman retrieved a huge, red leather-bound book for them. Frank opened it to see that it contained hundreds of deeds.

"It's unlawful to remove this book from the counter," Miss Beaumont said.

"That's fine." Frank leafed through the pages. Then he said to Miss Beaumont, "All these deeds look new." He pointed to one at random.

"It's dated 1938, but see? No wear and tear at all to the page."

Without looking up from her paperwork, Miss Beaumont snapped, "Fire."

"Fire?" said Joe.

"Recorder's office burned down about six years ago," said Miss Beaumont. Frank noticed that she seemed annoyed at having to share this information.

"And all the deeds were destroyed?" Joe asked.

"Every single one."

Frank came to the page that showed the titles to the land surrounding the national park. The deeds to the property were clearly registered in the name of Tyler Pardee.

"Who was county clerk six years ago?" Joe asked in a friendly voice.

"Martin Crowley," said Miss Beaumont. She peered up at them through her glasses. "Will that be all?"

"Yes, it will," answered Frank. "Thank you."

As they filed out of the courthouse, Jennifer hurried to keep up with Frank. "What does it all mean?" she demanded.

"It means," said Frank, "that you have to show us where Martin Crowley lived."

Martin Crowley's house was about five miles from the courthouse.

"I still don't know why we're here," Jennifer

said as she parked her car in front of Crowley's home.

"Because my brother has a hunch," Joe said good-naturedly. "Right, Frank?"

"More than a hunch," Frank said, hopping out of the car and walking up to the front door. He knocked and waited for an answer.

"I'm sure nobody's there," Jennifer told him. "Crowley lived alone."

"Wait here." Joe dashed around the side of the house. Frank waited, scanning the street to see whether anyone was watching. There was no one in sight.

Just then the front door opened. Joe stood there, grinning. "Welcome," he said.

Jennifer laughed and followed Frank inside. But Frank was all business as he ordered, "Spread out."

"What are we looking for?" asked Jennifer.

"Deeds," Frank told her.

Twenty minutes later Frank came out of a spare bedroom, waving a red book over his head. "What did I tell you?" he said triumphantly. "I found it at the top of the closet."

"What does it say?" asked Jennifer.

"Basically what I expected," answered Frank, holding it out for Joe to inspect.

But Joe was listening, his face still. "Uh-oh," he whispered. "We've got visitors."

Frank and Jennifer followed his gaze. Through

a front window, they spotted what they thought was the same blue pickup truck pulling slowly away from the front of the house. Its tinted windows prevented them from seeing who the driver was.

"As soon as it's past the front," Joe murmured, "we make a break for the car."

Just then, as though the driver had sensed he was being watched, the engine roared, and the pickup sped off.

"Go!" shouted Joe.

They ran for the car. This time Joe took the driver's seat, with Jennifer beside him in the passenger seat. Frank jumped over the side of the convertible into the back.

In seconds Joe had maneuvered the car in fast pursuit of the truck.

"Slow down!" Frank cautioned.

"I don't want to lose him," Joe retorted.

"Something's wrong," Frank shot back. "Why is he running from us all of a sudden? He was following us."

"That's what I want to find out," Joe answered, putting more pressure on the gas pedal.

"He disappeared around that turn!" cried Jennifer as they made their way into the countryside now.

Joe started to follow the truck around the turn, and as he pumped the brake pedal twice to slow the car slightly, he felt it go all the way to the floor.

The road not only was turning, it was going downhill now and the little convertible was picking up speed.

"Slow down, Joe!" Frank demanded.

"I can't!" Joe shouted. "The brakes are gone!"

Chapter

14

JENNIFER SCREAMED as the car tore down the hill.

Joe fought to keep the speeding vehicle on the road, but he felt he was losing the fight.

He tried to pull on the emergency brake, but there was too much speed built up. "The brake won't hold!" he shouted.

Joe had to focus all his attention on the road now.

At the bottom of the hill, the road formed a T intersection with another road. Across the intersection and dead ahead was the Tennessee River.

There were no guardrails running along the river, and Joe knew in an instant what would happen.

If he couldn't negotiate a turn—either left or right—they would plunge into the water.

"Get ready to jump if I don't make it!" he shouted.

The car raced forward.

The muscles in Joe's forearms began to ache from the strain of holding on to the steering wheel. I've got to hold on, he told himself grimly, gritting his teeth. All our lives depend on it!

At the bottom of the hill, Joe forced the steering wheel to the left until the car moved to the center of the road.

The car went into the turn with screeching tires. Joe could feel the right side of the car lift for a moment off the pavement.

At that instant, Joe pushed down on the accelerator. The sudden surge forward forced the wheels on the right side to drop back to the ground. To his triumph, he had control of the car again.

They were through the intersection! They had made it!

On the straightaway at the bottom of the hill, the car slowed enough for Joe to downshift, using the gears to bring down the speed. Finally Joe could control the car enough to steer it off the road and into some bushes, where it came to a complete stop.

"You did it, Joe." Frank congratulated him from the back of the car.

"Thanks, Joe," Jennifer said sincerely.

"I wouldn't want to do that every day," Joe admitted, already out of the car and sliding under it. "Frank, someone definitely cut the brake lines."

"It had to be," Frank said. "These perfectly timed accidents are turning into a pattern. The question now is, how do we get back from here."

"We've all got two legs, haven't we?" Jennifer said stoically. "My advice is, we walk."

"How much farther?" Joe groaned two hours later as they continued their stroll through the Tennessee countryside. It was the first really hot and humid day, and Joe could feel sweat trickling down his back and sides. He'd have given anything for a nice cold lemonade.

"About four miles," said Jennifer cheerfully. Unlike the Hardys, she seemed to be cool and comfortable.

"Why aren't there any cars on this road?" Joe asked.

"This is Tennessee, honey," Jennifer teased. "Not New York City."

As they kept walking, Joe glanced over at his brother. Frank had barely spoken during the entire walk. "Why so quiet, Frank?" Joe asked.

"I'm thinking about this book," he said, holding up the red book he had found at Crowley's house. "As soon as we get back, I want to talk to Robert Merriweather about it."

"Merriweather?" Joe was surprised. "Why him?"

"I need some information, and I think he can give it to me," Frank said.

Joe started to question him more, but then thought better of it. He sensed that Frank was reluctant to discuss the book in front of Jennifer.

Sure enough, Frank suggested that he and Joe go up to their room the moment they got back to the hotel.

"You're sure you'll be okay?" Joe said to Jennifer. "Your dad won't be too mad about your car, will he?"

"Why should he be?" said Jennifer bravely. "I wasn't the one who cut the brake lines." Her smile faded. "I'm not looking forward to explaining to him about the ammunition tent, though."

"Don't worry. I'll explain that to him myself," Joe assured her. Then he said goodbye to Jennifer and followed his brother upstairs.

"Okay, Frank," Joe said as soon as the two of them were alone in the room. "You didn't want to talk about the book in front of Jennifer. What's up?"

Frank looked embarrassed. "I didn't know I was so obvious," he said. "Listen, we don't know enough about these people, Joe. We have to be careful."

"So, what did you find?" Joe asked.

"The book contains a duplicate set of deeds," Frank said. "Or actually, not a duplicate, a different set. I'm not sure which book contains the genuine ones. I bet it's these, the ones from Crowley's house, but I won't be able to prove that right away, and we need to act fast."

"What do the deeds show?"

Frank leafed through the big book and said, "They indicate that while Tyler Pardee does own quite a bit of land around here, he doesn't own it all. Much of the property where Rebel Park is now—particularly the new section, where the new rides are going in and the corral is— belongs to several different people."

Frank pointed to a survey plot that showed tracts of land around the national park. Many tracts carried the name T. Pardee, but some others carried the names Hood, Colquist, and Langston.

"Maybe Pardee can explain this," Joe said doubtfully.

"Even if he can," said Frank, "it doesn't change the fact that Crowley was apparently up to something."

"But could that be a motive to kill him?"

"That's what we have to find out."

The Hardys didn't find Sheriff Walker until suppertime, when he approached them in the dining room. Frank saw him coming and silently pulled out a chair for the weary sheriff.

"Sorry I took so long getting to you, boys," the sheriff said, joining them. "It's been a busy day, what with the fire and all. I understand you were looking for me."

Frank smiled politely. He didn't intend to tell the sheriff about the brakes on Jennifer's car. He was sure the sheriff could find a way to dismiss it as just another accident—even though the lines had been cut—and Frank didn't feel he had the patience right then to deal with a reaction like that.

Instead, he filled the sheriff in on the book of deeds they found at Crowley's house and what it showed about who owned the land around the park. He also told him of his discovery that Dennis Kincaid was not a student at Tennessee State as he had claimed.

"Well," the sheriff drawled, "lying about being a student isn't exactly a crime."

"I knew you'd say that, Sheriff, and of course, you're right," Frank argued, "but with two murders on your hands I'd think the fact that somebody is lying about who he is might be of some importance."

The sheriff thought that over for a moment. Then he said, "Sorry, but nothing you've told me makes me disbelieve the fact that Wayne Robinson killed both men."

"Has he admitted to the murders?" Joe asked.

The sheriff smiled. "Not yet. But we expect he'll come around pretty soon."

He stood up. "Unless you boys have something else to tell me, I think I'll head home for some supper myself."

Frank frowned, stifling his anger. "Thank you, Sheriff," he said.

"Stay in touch," the sheriff said, and walked away.

"Yeah, Sheriff," Joe said. "Thanks for nothing," he finished under his breath.

But Frank had already gone on to the next step in his plan. "After supper," he said to Joe, "let's stop by the front desk to see if we can find Dennis Kincaid."

"Fine," Joe mumbled between forkfuls of food. "Just let me get this down first. Walking for miles in the middle of nowhere helps a guy work up an appetite."

After supper Joe accompanied Frank to the front desk, where they learned that Dennis Kincaid had checked out. "Did you get a home address, by any chance?" Frank asked the young clerk.

"I'll check." The clerk thumbed through the registration forms. "Yeah, here it is. The address is in Lowryville. That's about ten miles east of here."

"Great," Frank said, waving his gratitude to the clerk and turning away from the desk. "Now that we know where to find Dennis, let's get upstairs to find Merriweather.''

Joe was surprised to see, when Robert Merriweather answered the door of his room, that the assistant was obviously packing. His suitcase was open on the bed and half filled with a package wrapped in brown paper.

"Going somewhere?" he asked Merriweather.

"I'm checking out tomorrow. My flight's in the evening, but I like to get my packing started early. Not that it's really any of your business."

Both Joe and Frank were surprised. "I assumed we were going back together," Frank said. "Why didn't you tell us you'd changed your plans?"

For the first time since they had met him, Merriweather lost his temper. "I don't have to tell you anything," he snapped, red-faced. "Your plans were with the professor. The professor's dead. What I do is none of your business, and vice versa for that matter."

"Look, I just want to ask you a couple of questions," Frank said, trying to edge his way past the door. "Would it be okay to talk to you for just a couple of minutes?"

"What about?"

Frank held up the red book of deeds. Merriweather's face registered shock when he saw it, and his familiar nervousness returned. He stepped back into the room and sat, stunned, on the bed.

Finally he spoke. "What do you want from me?"

"It seems you've seen this book before," Frank said calmly.

"No," said Merriweather, trying to look aloof. "Should I have?"

"You tell us," said Joe.

"Tell you what?"

Frank stepped forward. "Why was the professor interested in who owned the land around the park?"

"I've already told you I don't know."

"Might he have been planning to use the information against Crowley?" Frank persisted.

Merriweather became extremely annoyed now. "Look, I don't mind answering questions when you're asking me something I know about, but since you aren't, I'll have to ask you to leave."

Merriweather stood up and walked toward the door.

Joe hesitated, but Frank reluctantly cooperated. "Thanks, Robert," he said as he passed him on his way out the door. "You've been a big help."

"What a grouch," Joe grumbled as the door closed behind both brothers.

"Don't worry about it." Joe noticed that Frank was surprisingly cheerful. "We won't have to talk to him much anymore. I could stand a little relaxation. How about showing me Rebel Park?"

* * *

It was almost closing time when the Hardys entered the gates of the amusement park. Joe noted that there were very few people inside.

"We probably have time for only one ride," Joe said. "You want to try the best one?"

"Sure." Frank smiled. "What's the best ride?"

"Well, if you forget the new tilt-a-whirl, which I suggest you do," Joe said, steering his brother down the midway, "then the best ride is definitely the Rebel Yell roller coaster. Jennifer says it's famous all over Tennessee, and it's the first ride her dad put up on this land."

The boys hurried down the length of the midway to the large roller coaster, which stood a short distance away from the other rides. Joe glanced up at it, noticing how it gleamed in the moonlight. When the ticket taker told them this would be the last ride of the night, Joe was relieved. Despite his love of excitement, he wasn't crazy about amusement park rides.

An instant after Frank and Joe fastened themselves into their seats, the ride began, even though they were the only passengers.

The first curves and loops were tame, but as the inclines became steeper and steeper the roller coaster gathered speed. Joe held on tight, so caught up in the fury of the ride that he didn't even notice the first gunshot.

"What was that?" Frank said, startled.

"What?" shouted Joe over the screeching of the roller coaster.

Just then, a second bullet ricocheted off the metal railing near Joe's head, causing him to duck instantly.

"Company!" he yelled at his brother.

Frank and Joe turned cautiously to look behind them.

Sitting four cars behind them was a masked gunman.

He stared at Joe, lifted his gun, and took careful aim.

Chapter

15

"LOOK OUT!" Joe pushed Frank's head down toward the seat and ducked down himself, just as the gunman fircd a third shot and then a fourth.

Aiming a gun on a roller coaster couldn't be easy, Joe assured himself, but when he peered over the top of the car he saw that the gunman had moved down and was now only three cars from the Hardys.

"You okay?" he shouted to Frank over the noise of the ride.

"Yeah. You?"

"So far. Any ideas?"

"There's always prayer."

Joe peeked over the edge again. Now the masked man was only two cars away. The roller coaster swooped into a long, graceful curve and the gunman raised his revolver once again.

Joe wondered who the gunman could be. It was impossible to tell with a red bandanna and sunglasses covering his face. While he was wondering the gunman fired again, missing him by mere inches this time.

Joe ducked lower down into the car.

Joe kept his head down, knowing that the gunman would have a perfectly clear shot if he rose up. Joe hung on to the seat next to Frank, feeling the car lurch into a steep uphill climb.

He heard a cry behind them.

"What's that?" he asked.

"How should I know?" shouted Frank.

Unable to resist a peek, Joe stuck his head back over the edge of the car.

The gunman had fallen backward in his seat! Even better, he'd dropped his gun! He was staring over the edge of the car at the ground, where Joe saw what he guessed was the revolver lying fifty feet below.

"It's our turn now!" cried Joe as he stood up and started climbing back toward the shooter.

"Careful, Joe!" Frank yelled.

The roller coaster was careening madly from one curve to another now, but Joe ignored the wild tosses as he climbed seat by seat toward the gunman, who was running from him as fast as he could.

Joe grabbed the guardrail just in time as the roller coaster zoomed downhill. Just a few more seats now, he told himself. You're doing fine.

But a moment later the roller coaster went into another slow uphill climb. Joe leapt over the last few seats toward the masked man, but his quarry was able to leap down onto the track behind the train and half slide, half climb down the track to safety.

"I can't believe it!" Joe slammed his hand down on the back of the last seat. Wearily he turned to climb back toward Frank, who sat watching from the front.

"Good job," Frank muttered to his brother as the two of them climbed, weak-kneed, off the ride.

They agreed to call the sheriff in the morning. That night they didn't feel up to the man's skepticism.

The next morning the brothers awoke to a horrendous rain storm. Frank rolled over and immediately dialed the sheriff's office but was told the sheriff would have to return his call.

"Bad weather for a day trip," Joe remarked, remembering they had to drive to Lowryville to look for Dennis Kincaid.

"Neither rain nor hail nor dark of night, old buddy," said Frank, climbing out of bed. "Come on, get dressed. I'll meet you downstairs for breakfast."

Frank made a point of checking the brakes on the professor's rental car before they took it on the road.

Joe drove, and once they were on their way, with the windshield wipers going and the radio on low, he leaned back against the seat and said, "Okay, partner, you've got a theory. Start talking."

"Not a theory, really. Just a bunch of bits and pieces so far."

"Out with it," Joe insisted.

"Okay," Frank said. "For starters, we know from the sheriff that the same gun, and therefore it could be argued that the same person, killed both the professor and Martin Crowley. That has to rule Crowley out as the professor's killer."

"That makes sense." Joe grinned.

"My first assumption was that the professor was blackmailing Crowley in some way over the different land deeds."

"And now?"

Frank said, "Now I'm not so sure. As soon as we get back from seeing our good friend Kincaid, I want to meet with Tyler Pardee and hear what he has to say about the deeds."

"What else have you got?" asked Joe.

"A bunch of little things. We know Kincaid isn't really a student, but that fact isn't such a big deal. We also know that Crowley wanted to tell us something right before he was shot."

"And we know that Robert Merriweather has been wrought up about something the whole time he's been here," Joe said. "That's it?"

"That's it," Frank admitted. "It may not sound like much, but I think it tells it all."

Frank and Joe discovered that the town of Lowryville consisted of little more than a single row of houses and a gas station. Frank easily learned the location of Kincaid's house by asking the gas station attendant.

He studied the little house through the pouring rain. It would probably look almost as bleak on a sunny day, he decided. The walls were made of unpainted wood and the roof was tin. An old dog crouched on the front porch, trying to keep out of the rain but not having much luck.

"Look." Frank nodded toward a blue pickup truck parked in the gravel driveway. Its right front fender and headlight were smashed. Frank knew they hadn't been broken the day before.

"This must be the place," Joe remarked. "But when did Kincaid smash his truck up? I hope he did it when he almost killed us."

"We'd better be extra careful," Frank cautioned. "Kincaid may be dangerous."

The Hardys dashed through the rain to the house, while the dog barked loudly but made no effort to move.

Frank knocked on the door, and a pretty young woman in a cotton dress answered. She was holding a tiny baby.

"Dennis," the woman called out, not taking her eyes off the dripping boys. "Company."

She silently motioned the Hardys inside. Frank followed her in, peering through the dim light at the cluttered but clean and cozy little living room. Joe entered behind him just as Dennis Kincaid appeared from a back room.

Frank eyed the young man's self-satisfied smile as he greeted the Hardys. He didn't introduce the woman, who disappeared into the back room with the baby.

"So," he said, "the great detectives track me down at last. What tipped you off? The fact that I charged my room at the hotel?" he said sarcastically.

Frank sensed that Joe was having a hard time controlling his anger. "It was you in the truck!" Joe yelled.

Kincaid sat down on a lumpy sofa and grinned. "I registered at the hotel with my real address because I couldn't care less if you found me," he said. "I have nothing to hide and nothing to say. Looks like you boys got wet for nothing."

"Why did you lie about being a student?" Frank asked.

Kincaid glared at him from the sofa. "You think I'm not smart enough to go to college. I have the smarts. I just don't have the bucks."

"Did you try for a scholarship," Joe asked sarcastically.

"Yeah, right," snarled Kincaid, half-rising. "Why don't you just get out of here?"

"Okay." Frank was worried that if they didn't

leave soon, his brother and Kincaid would get in a fight. "We've seen enough."

"But we need to make him talk," Joe protested.

"You and who else?" taunted Kincaid.

"Come on, Joe," Frank insisted, guiding his brother toward the door. "Let's go."

It rained even harder as Frank and Joe drove back to Magnolia House. Joe was still angry, so Frank took a turn at the wheel.

"He nearly killed us with that truck of his," Joe seethed as they neared the hotel.

"But we can't prove that," Frank answered. "There are lots of blue pickups, and we never saw his with that smashed-up fender before." He tried to sound calm and mask his own anger.

"Maybe not," Joe retorted. "But we both know it's true."

The Magnolia House gate swung into sight, opening instantly as Frank turned the car onto the private drive. He wondered why Pardee had bothered putting up this gate if it opened whenever any car approached it.

Jennifer was waiting in the foyer when they returned. "There you are," she said as the boys, still damp, ran in through the big, double front doors. "I thought you might have driven out to look for Kincaid today. Did you find him?"

"The less said about that, the better," Frank remarked. "Jennifer, can you take us to your father?"

Both Jennifer and Joe were surprised. "Sure," Jennifer said. "He's upstairs. Follow me."

Tyler Pardee was sitting at the desk in his third-floor office. Jennifer showed them inside and then left the Hardys alone with her father.

"Come in, come in," he said expansively as the boys entered. "What can I do for you?" He motioned generously for the boys to sit.

"We'll be brief, Mr. Pardee," said Frank. "We've come to ask you a few questions about the deeds to the land around here."

Frank watched Pardee's face carefully, but the man's expression remained blank. "What's on your mind?" Pardee asked pleasantly.

"Well, to put it bluntly," Frank began, "we discovered a duplicate set of books in Crowley's house, and they show that you don't own all the land that the deeds in the courthouse claim you do."

Pardee nodded and smiled. "Those old books. Of course you're confused. You see, Martin was a history buff himself, and he kept those useless deeds as a memento. They're interesting, I suppose, but they carry no legal weight. The ones in the courthouse are the genuine article. Anything else?"

Before Frank or Joe could answer, Pardee's secretary buzzed him and he picked up his phone.

"Yes?" Pardee said. He listened in silence, but Frank saw that he was growing angrier by the moment. "Well, Mr.—" He stopped when he remembered the Hardys. "Remember, my friend," he said into the phone in a whisper, "that my daughter nearly got hurt in that little incident. You went too far, and you can pay to fix your own fender."

Pardee put down the phone and apologized. "Now, where were we?"

"Actually," said Frank, "I think we're all done."

Pardee stood up, obviously relieved. "Well, then, glad I could be of some help."

"Thank you, sir," Joe said, shaking Pardee's hand before he followed his brother out into the hall.

"Tyler Pardee hired Kincaid to stop us?" he questioned Frank the minute they were out of earshot of the office.

"It looks that way," said Frank.

"We have to talk to the sheriff," said Joe. "Let's check to see if he's called us back yet."

Frank was about to agree when they both heard someone shouting. Dreading what might be happening now, they moved quickly to the top of the stairs.

"Fire!" someone was shouting. "Get out! The hotel's on fire!"

Chapter

16

JOE RACED AHEAD of Frank to the foyer, where a crowd was gathering.

"What's going on?" Joe asked a bellhop who was racing by.

"There's a fire in one of the rooms upstairs, and it's spreading fast," the bellboy answered.

"Which room?" Frank demanded.

"Room two forty-five," the bellhop shouted as he ran on.

"That's the professor's room!" cried Frank. "There must be something in it we missed. It's no coincidence that the fire started there."

The Hardys ran quickly up one flight of stairs.

As soon as Joe reached the top of the stairs, he could see smoke billowing out from beneath a set of double doors that closed off the far half of the corridor. "Looks like we may be too late, Frank," he told his brother.

Frank shook his head. "I want to be sure."

He spotted a small fire extinguisher on the wall near the staircase. "Wait here," he said. "If I'm gone longer than two minutes, come after me."

Frank flung open the heavy double doors, and a thick, black cloud of smoke billowed out onto the landing. The smoke burned Joe's eyes and made him cough. He realized after a few moments that he wasn't positive how long Frank had been gone.

He took a few steps back down the stairs to get away from the smoke, which was rolling out from under the doors now. Downstairs, Joe heard the fire trucks arrive. Fire fighters began evacuating anyone left in the hotel.

It's been at least two minutes, Joe told himself. I'm going after him.

Just as Joe reached for the handle of the door, Frank stumbled out, followed by a dense cloud of smoke. His eyes were closed and tears were streaming down his face. He was coughing and could hardly speak.

"Couldn't—I couldn't get through," he gasped. "The smoke was too thick—"

"Take it easy, Frank," Joe said, guiding him down the stairs. "Whatever was in there is destroyed now."

Outside, they joined the other guests and

watched the fire fighters. Joe was glad to let professionals take over.

A couple of hours later the fire was extinguished. All the guests—except those in the professor's wing—were allowed back into their rooms. Joe and Frank ran gratefully to their room.

"I can't believe the whole building didn't burn down," Frank commented. "The smoke in the professor's room was incredible."

"Well, it probably destroyed every single thing in there," Joe pointed out, "but this is a sturdy old house. Built to last."

Frank was reaching for the telephone to try the sheriff again when it rang. Frank answered.

"Hello. A message for Joe Hardy?" The voice was that of one of the hotel clerks. "Miss Pardee has asked to meet him at the hall of mirrors in twenty minutes, please."

"Twenty minutes," Frank repeated, smiling. "Thanks. I'll tell him."

He hung up the phone.

"Tell me what?" Joe asked. "That the fire in the professor's room was the result of arson? That much I already figured."

"Nope. Better than that," Frank said with a smile. "Miss Pardee has requested your presence in twenty minutes at the illustrious hall of mirrors."

Joe sat up. "The hall of mirrors? It's raining outside."

Frank shrugged. "I'm only the messenger." Then he grinned. "Chivalry may not be dead, but it's about to get very wet."

"Funny," said Joe. "Very funny."

After Joe had gone to meet Jennifer at Rebel Park, Frank lay down on his bed and thought through the case again. Suddenly he sat up—he knew who committed the murders and why. The memory that triggered the solution was the one of Robert Merriweather packing. It was the package wrapped in brown paper on top of the man's suitcase. The case made sense now—he just needed proof and a look at that package to verify his suspicions. He called the sheriff again.

"I understand he's busy," Frank said in growing frustration to the officer who answered, "but I have to speak to him soon. It's urgent." He paused. "I'll hold, thanks."

Frank hummed to himself as he gazed out the window. Rain continued to pound against the glass.

"Sheriff Walker," came a voice over the phone.

"Sheriff, hi. It's Frank Hardy."

"What can I do for you, son?"

"It's Robert Merriweather. He's at the airport now, and you have to stop him. It's vital—he holds the key to the whole investigation."

There was a spluttering sound coming over the wires. "Now, look here, son," came the sheriff's voice. "I've tried to be patient with you and your brother, but the airport isn't in my jurisdiction." The sheriff was ready to hang up.

"I know that, Sheriff." Frank forced himself to remain calm. "But we're talking about murder here—"

"I've got my murderer," the sheriff snapped. "Wayne Robinson's been formally charged."

"Sheriff, I promise you that Merriweather is carrying evidence that will prove who murdered both Professor Donnell and Martin Crowley," Frank said, crossing his fingers against the slight possibility he was wrong. "Do you have that kind of evidence against Wayne Robinson?"

The sheriff paused and seemed to consider what Frank said. "I'll make a call," the sheriff said finally.

"Can you get him here to Magnolia House along with Kincaid?" Frank asked, knowing he might be pushing his luck. "Also we need Merriweather's luggage," Frank added.

"Well, I hope you're right about all this," the sheriff said resignedly.

"Thanks," Frank said.

Just as Frank hung up the phone, he heard a knock at the door.

It was Jennifer Pardee.

"Well, this is a surprise," said Frank.

"I know." Jennifer smiled. "I'm inviting you both for dinner. My treat."

Frank was confused. "Why aren't you at the hall of mirrors?" he asked.

"In this rain?" said Jennifer. "Are you kidding?"

"But Joe got your message," Frank insisted. He was beginning to get a terrible feeling in his stomach.

"What message?"

"To meet him in the hall of mirrors!" Frank was already moving past her into the corridor. "He's been gone over an hour. How do I get there?"

"Wait for me." Jennifer ran to keep up with him.

"Just tell me how to get there," insisted Frank as the two of them ran down the stairs. "Is it near the roller coaster?"

"Right beside it." Jennifer ran to the front desk and grabbed a raincoat. "But I'm coming, too."

"You call the sheriff's office," Frank ordered, heading for the front doors. "Tell Walker to get some deputies to meet me at the hall as soon as possible. Tell him it's a matter of life and death."

Jennifer tossed the raincoat to Frank.

"Then go to your room and stay there with the door locked. Don't open it for anyone except me, Joe, or the sheriff."

"What about—"

Frank was firm. "Me, Joe, or the sheriff. No exceptions. None."

Jennifer wavered. "Okay, I'll do it. But hurry!"

As Frank was running out into the rain, Joe was studying five different versions of himself, all of them wet, angry, and confused.

Joe took a careful step to the left. Now there were only three of him.

He had never liked halls of mirrors, but this day would go down as one of his all-time bad hall-of-mirrors experiences.

He was mad that Jennifer hadn't shown up. Thinking Frank might have gotten the message wrong, he'd taken a quick walk around the park to see if he could spot her, but that had proved fruitless.

In fact, thanks to the rain, there was practically no one in Rebel Park. Everyone else has enough sense to stay in out of the rain, Joe realized gloomily.

Finally, he had returned to the hall of mirrors hoping that Jennifer had just been delayed. At least it's inside, he thought, comforting himself. He felt very wet and alone now, though.

Just then he heard a door open and close. It sounded like the door on the far side of the building.

"Jennifer? Is that you? It's me, Joe. Over here." Joe glanced in front of him and laughed.

"I'm not sure where 'here' is, actually, but there are three of me, if that helps."

There was no answer. Joe began to worry. "Who's there?" he demanded.

The distinct click of a revolver being cocked sent chills down his spine. He heard a man's voice say very clearly, "When your brother gets here—and I'm sure he'll come—he'll find you dead. And he'll be next."

As Frank reached the entrance to the hall of mirrors the storm reached its peak. A bolt of lightning flashed through the sky, followed immediately by a huge clap of thunder.

Or was that gunfire?

Frank rushed inside, shouting, "Joe! Are you in here?"

"Frank!"

Frank was relieved to hear Joe's voice. But then his relief faded.

"Be careful!" Joe was shouting. "It's Pardee! He's got a gun!"

Chapter

17

FRANK WAS GRATEFUL for his martial arts training as he moved through the dimly lit hall. Martial arts had taught him to be light on his feet—and to control his fear.

In a flash Frank thought he saw Pardee. Instinctively, he stepped back. In the next instant, a shot rang out, and glass crashed all around Frank.

I can't stay in here unarmed, Frank realized. "Joe, stay down," he yelled, and ran back outside to get something, anything, to use as a weapon.

He instantly spotted a stand with stacks of baseballs. He took off and filled his raincoat pockets with as many balls as he could carry.

Back inside the hall of mirrors, Frank announced, "Joe, I'm back. Stay down."

Standing half-hidden in the doorway of the spooky hall, Frank methodically pitched baseballs at the mirrors, smashing them one by one and ducking back after each toss.

"You're not going to stop me with those," warned Pardee.

Over the noise of the storm came the distinct whine of sirens as police cars entered the park. Frank kept silent but threw a ball in the direction of Pardee's voice. Another huge mirror smashed to pieces. Behind where it had been stood Tyler Pardee.

"Give it up, sir," Frank said in a level voice. "It's over. The police are here."

Pardee didn't answer but only raised his gun and aimed at Frank.

Suddenly Joe appeared out of the darkness. As Frank watched, he flew a few feet to tackle Pardee from behind. The gun slipped out of the hotel owner's hand and skidded across the floor.

Frank snatched up the gun. "You can let him up, Joe. I've got him covered."

Just as Joe stepped back from the man, Sheriff Walker pushed past Frank into the shattered hall. "What's going on here?" he demanded as half a dozen deputies followed him inside.

Frank turned Pardee's gun over to Walker with a weary smile. "Sir, that's a story I'd like to tell."

*   *   *

After the Hardys had showered and changed into dry clothes, they took off for the library, where everyone was gathered.

Frank knew that the sheriff's colleagues had been able to stop Robert Merriweather at the airport. Merriweather would be waiting in the library, along with Dennis Kincaid.

As the Hardys walked down the corridor, Joe said, "What bothers me most is Jennifer."

"I know." Frank frowned. "This has to be awful for her."

"I wish there was something I could do."

"Not much you can do except be her friend."

Frank was pleased to see a guard posted outside the library. The guard opened the door, and the Hardys stepped inside.

Frank saw Tyler Pardee, Jennifer, Robert Merriweather, and Kincaid seated around the library table in the center of the room. The package wrapped in brown paper lay on top of the table.

Sheriff Walker, who stood in one corner of the room, brightened when the Hardys entered. "Good. Now maybe we can get to the bottom of this," he said.

Joe took a seat next to Jennifer, but to his disappointment she ignored him. Frank remained standing. "I think we can," he told the sheriff. "Is that the package from Robert's suitcase?" He gestured toward the package on the table.

"That's it," the sheriff confirmed.

Frank tore the paper off the manuscript and

read what he assumed the title would be. "*Southern Carpetbaggers: A Sad Legacy of the Confederacy.*"

He put the manuscript back on the table. "You see," he began, "Crowley knew that not all carpetbaggers came down from the North. He'd been blackmailing Tyler Pardee for years after he'd discovered that the Pardee family didn't really hold fair title to all the land they claimed."

"Is that so, Tyler?" said the sheriff.

Pardee looked at the table. "Talk to my lawyer," he said sullenly.

"My guess is," Frank continued, glancing at his brother for support, "that Crowley's demands weren't so great and Pardee didn't mind paying him off to keep him quiet."

"He tried to get Wayne Robinson elected," Joe put in despite Jennifer's obvious discomfort, "so he could get Robinson to find the real book of deeds and destroy it once and for all. By the way, Sheriff, the real book is hidden in our room upstairs. We pried up a few floorboards."

The sheriff nodded. "Go on."

"After Crowley was reelected, I'm sure his price went up," said Frank. "But otherwise everything was business as usual until the professor and Merriweather started researching the professor's new book."

Frank pulled a note out of his pocket. "Merriweather says he never saw this note, but don't believe him. It asks Merriweather to check into who owns the land around here. See where this corner's been torn off? That's where the professor dated his notes. I think Merriweather tore off the date so he could deny having seen it. Obviously the note was old—from when Donnell was doing his research for *Carpetbaggers*."

"Why wouldn't he just destroy the note?" asked the sheriff.

"Probably because he was afraid Frank or I had already seen it and might get even more suspicious if it disappeared," Joe offered.

"Once Merriweather found out that Pardee really didn't own the land, he began blackmailing him, too. But Merriweather's most brilliant move," Frank continued, "was in convincing Pardee that it was actually the professor who was blackmailing him."

"Hold on a minute," said the sheriff. "It may be true that Tyler's people took land from their neighbors, but that happened a lot in the South. Families often ran when fighting broke out and just never came back. It's not the biggest crime in the world."

"No, it isn't," Frank agreed. "That's probably why Crowley wasn't able to gouge Pardee for too much. But the professor was a world-famous author, and I don't think the National Park Service would take kindly to a southern carpetbagger running a theme park and a profitable Battle of Shiloh reenactment next to a national historic site. Pardee felt he had to kill him.''

For a moment the room was deadly quiet.

Then Jennifer said to Frank, "If what you say is true about my dad—and I don't believe it for a minute—explain why he would intentionally try to harm me. Joe and I were attacked in the tunnel of love. And you, Joe, and I nearly died when the brakes on my car were cut.''

Frank gave Jennifer a sympathetic look. "I'm afraid those two incidents are what started me thinking your father *did* do it.''

"Explain that one,'' said the sheriff.

"Pardee had hired Kincaid to frighten—only frighten—Jennifer and me, knowing that that would divert any possible attention from him,'' Joe said. "As for the brakes going out, Frank and I overheard Pardee talking to Kincaid about that one. He said he'd gone too far. I don't think he cared if Frank or I got hurt or even killed—we'd be out of his way.''

"So you're saying it was Kincaid who killed the professor and Crowley?'' asked the sheriff.

"No.'' Frank tried to be patient. "Kincaid only harassed us. He drove that truck at the airport. He knocked Joe down the stairs. He set fire to the ammo tent and knocked the wall out of the barn. He drove the wild horses at Joe and me, and he shot at us on the roller coaster, I'm sure. But only one person could sneak live ammo onto the battlefield: Tyler Pardee.''

"But you found a box of live ammo in the supply room yourself," the sheriff protested.

"Yes, because it was planted there by Pardee to make it look like a random bullet killed the professor."

"And the fire in Donnell's room?" asked the sheriff. "Pardee or Kincaid?"

"Neither," said Joe. "Merriweather did that."

"Why?" asked the sheriff in surprise.

"He wanted to destroy any evidence that might link him to the blackmailing."

The sheriff shook his head. "It makes for an interesting story, boys, but I'm not sure it'll stand up in court."

"You're forgetting ballistics," Frank replied. "I'm certain if you test Pardee's rifle against the bullets that killed the professor and Crowley, you'll find that they match."

"That reminds me, Frank," said Joe. "If Pardee didn't have a real problem with Crowley, why bother to kill him? Everybody was ready to call the professor's death an accident."

"Good question, Joe. I think he saw how easy it was to deal with the professor, and he figured he could make Crowley's death look accidental, too. And don't forget, people saw Crowley saying he had something to tell us. I'm sure that got back to Pardee, and he felt he had to act."

"What about the book about Beauregard?" the sheriff wanted to know.

"Oh, he was working on that one, all right,

but it wasn't the trouble spot. This one was, and this one was finished," Frank said.

"I've heard enough," said the sheriff. "Deputy, take these three men to jail. We'll deal with the charges when I get there." All three men were as silent leaving the room as they had been the past fifteen minutes.

The sheriff turned to Frank and Joe. "I guess I owe you two an apology. And thanks."

"Don't mention it." Frank exchanged an uneasy smile with his brother. "Any time."

Joe was packed and ready to go early the next morning. Their flight left at eight o'clock, and he wanted time for a snack at the airport. As he and Frank loaded their bags into the rental car in front of the mansion, Joe heard Jennifer call.

"Joe, wait!"

Joe flushed, stuffing his garment bag in faster. He had been unable to sleep most of the night, worrying about Jennifer and how she was taking the news about her father—and finally how she felt about the fact that he had helped put her dad behind bars. He had almost called her to say how sorry he was but had held back.

Now he felt as though he had been caught trying to run away. Which, of course, he was.

"Your problem, little brother," Frank said sympathetically. He climbed into the car and closed the door.

Joe turned to face the red-haired girl. "I'm

sorry, Jennifer," he said. "It's not the way I wanted things to turn out."

"Me, either." There were tears in her beautiful green eyes. "But you didn't do anything wrong. I know that." She hesitated, blushing. "Will I ever see you again?"

Joe couldn't believe his ears. Had Jennifer forgiven him? "I—I hope so," he stammered.

"I hope so, too," she said. "I mean it." Smiling tearfully at him, she took his hand.

They looked at each other for a moment. Then Joe dropped her hand and closed the lid of the trunk. "I'd better be going," he said.

"Write to me, okay?" said Jennifer, stepping back out of the way.

He grinned and nodded, then climbed into the car.

"You'd better wipe that smile off your face, little brother," Frank said as he pulled the car away.

Joe shot him a questioning look.

"Our job down here may be over, but we still have to write a paper for English, figure out the hit-miss ratio for math, and—"

"Enough, enough!" Joe shouted, putting his hands over his ears.

The brothers laughed. Then Frank turned to look one last time at the green, rolling fields of Shiloh.

Frank and Joe's next case:

The Hardys are working security on the set of the latest film in a cult classic series, *Horror House V*. Frank and Joe get the chance to appear on-screen as victims of the movie's psycho murderer—the dreaded Reaper. But the fake fun soon turns to true terror when producer Andrew Warmouth meets a death as horrible as anything captured on film!

The movie is being shot on location at an actual haunted house, and the ghastly truth behind the murder is buried within. The investigation leads Frank and Joe into a living nightmare: They must face their worst fears and track down an elusive, cold-blooded killer before he strikes again . . . in *Web of Horror*, Case #53 in The Hardy Boys Casefiles™.